The Alter Ego ... mm
by Penny Hart-Woods

Penny Hart-Woods.

Text © 2014 Penny Hart-Woods

Penny Hart-Woods asserts the moral right to be identified as the author of this work.

Published by Hartlington Press
www.hartlingtonpress.co.uk

A catalogue record for this book is available from the British Library.

ISBN: 978-0-9929199-3-1

Typeset in Meridien.

Printed and bound in Great Britain by Hart & Clough Ltd.

To my wonderful partner and
my extraordinarily brilliant friends.

Table Of Contents

1

Realisation

We are always told that change starts with a single step.

No matter how big or small that change is to be, there comes a time when you just have to stop thinking and take the plunge.

So it was with me.

I'm not entirely sure when the penny finally dropped. Perhaps it was the morning I came downstairs and found the kitchen empty, as usual, the remnants of a breakfast for two laying messily before me.

There had been no cheery goodbye from my husband or daughter, no affectionate kiss on the cheek as they went out the door; they had left the house to go about their business of the day without even giving me a thought.

As I sat and drank my first cup of coffee, I found and began to read the list of instructions I had been left for the day.

Husband needed: 4 clean shirts to be packed and pressed for a business trip he was taking the next day. He also wanted a lift to the airport, the car putting in for a service whilst he was gone, and new batteries for his toothbrush.

Daughter required: clean games kit for Thursday, picking up late after school because she had hockey practice and the following list of ingredients for her Home Economics class tomorrow:

- 200g corn flour
- 300g plain flour, plus more as needed
- 1 teaspoon baking powder
- 1/2 teaspoon baking soda

- 1/4 teaspoon fine salt
- 8 tablespoons unsalted butter at room temperature
- 100g granulated sugar
- 2 large egg yolks
- 1 tablespoon Pisco or brandy
- 1/2 teaspoon vanilla extract
- 1 cup Dulce de Leche, at room temperature
- Icing sugar, for dusting

I read the list again. Dulce de Leche? What the hell was that, and more to the point how on earth was I going to get some by tomorrow morning?

Bloody Home Ec teacher, does she not realise we live in the middle of sodding nowhere? The nearest thing we have to a large shop is a Spar five miles away and the closest they get to exotic cuisine is pork pie with apple sauce on top. How on earth does she expect us to come up with this kind of stuff at short notice?

I considered calling the school and making suitably angry protestations, but settled instead for googling said item.

Turned out it was some kind of cream filling for cakes or biscuits that you made using condensed milk. Once the recipe was found, I set about making it.

Two and a half hours later, having had to learn and master the art of oven cooking using the bain-marie method, I had a bowl of what I proudly discerned looked very much like the melted fudgy mess that was in the picture.

I spent the remainder of the day completing my list of tasks, a quick detour to the village shop for toothbrush batteries and I could head straight on to school to get Rebecca.

"Another day done," I said to myself. "Another day filled with all the excitement and challenge of squeezing a hot tea bag with your fingers. Oh, but hang on a minute, Marjorie be still your beating heart, how could you have forgotten the daily ritual of what to make for dinner? How could you possibly be down hearted when you still have that prospect to relish and be joyful about? One of these days I'm going to serve up fish fingers and chips, just to see the look of horror on George's face!"

I set off to drive the six miles to Rebecca's school. It was dusk and the fall of light drizzle made the hills and trees I passed seem dark and oppressive.

"Bloody countryside, why on earth did we ever move here? It never stops bloody raining, there's no such thing as bloody summer and you have to drive 15 bloody miles to get to a bloody supermarket! George Primm, I hate you," I shouted. "You're an arse and I will never forgive you!"

I pulled up outside school and saw Rebecca stood in the bus shelter. She was with a group of her friends laughing and messing about. Her demeanour immediately changed when she saw the car. Gone was the smile and back was the teenage pout. She walked over and got in the back.

"You're late," she snapped.

"I don't think so darling," I said defensively. "You said quarter past and it's only 18 minutes past."

"That's three minutes mother, three minutes of me getting wet that shouldn't have happened."

"Well, I'm very sorry dear." I was ridiculously apologetic. "There are road works on the A57, traffic control and all that, perhaps that's why."

"Yeah, yeah, whatever, can we just go home now?"

She promptly put on headphones and plugged into her iPod. As far as she was concerned, that was the end of the matter.

I set off to drive home, livid with myself for allowing this 13 year old child to speak to me in the way that she did. It wasn't the first time either. It was happening all the time now.

I had put it down to hormones, the inevitable onset of puberty that every parent dreads, but in truth Rebecca's attitude was starting to become indistinguishable from George's; it was like having a mini version of him around all the time.

"You're so boring Mummy," she had said a few days earlier. The tone of her voice was patronizing and offensive. "Catherine Barker's mum is so awesome. She's an artist and sculptor and is about to have her own exhibition in Leeds next month. You, you can't do anything like that, can you?"

I remember making some kind of sorry excuse along the lines of: "Well, not everyone can be talented, can they?" and had left the room feeling annoyed and hurt.

Go and live with amazing Mrs bloody painter then if she's so awesome. Let's just see how long she can remain exciting and wonderful when she's looking after a belligerent, selfish little girl that has OCD tendencies about her teddy collection.

I spent the evening feeling sorry for myself, imagining all these high powered mums spending their days alternating between heading up multinational corporations and doing good works for the local community. They no doubt still had time to prepare Cordon Bleu dinners for their husbands and make outstanding costumes for the school play.

Bitches! Why does everyone else have to be so bloody perfect?

The bitter memories of how I had tried, but always failed to be accepted into the school mummy circle came back to me with surprising intensity. This 'set' was so cliquey, I would have had more chance of breaking into 'The Masons' than becoming part of their elitist group.

I never got invitations to coffee mornings or girlie nights out and was definitely never included in the weekly group classes for Zumba or Pilates. I was an outsider and I never understood why.

Fortunately for Rebecca this did not affect her making friends. She, happily, was a confident, outgoing, intelligent girl who was always in demand.

Of course, there was a time when I was the most wonderful person in her life. I remembered when my finger painting skills were bragged about at the nursery gates and my home made play-doh was the sought after recipe of all mums. But now she had forgotten all the brilliant things we had done together. My little girl was growing up. I was losing her respect and probably deservedly so.

I finally concluded that the real reason I was so angry was because I knew she was right. I was boring; I didn't ever do anything.

I put the events of that night behind me and concentrated on the drive home. The rain was heavier now; night had closed in and the dusky grey of the hills was a dark black outline against the skyline. God, it was so depressing.

We arrived home and I noticed George's car in the drive. He was a little earlier than usual, which meant he would want his dinner sooner rather than later.

Rebecca went straight to find her dad and I could hear them laughing in his study. I went straight to the kitchen to make dinner.

The meal itself was an uneventful affair. We ate as always in the kitchen; the ritual of the dining room was reserved for special occasions.

"Why have a dining room and not use it?" I had once questioned George.

"Because Marjorie, it is for special occasions only, entertaining and parties etc."

"But we don't have parties or entertain, George," I had said.

"No, dear, we don't. That's because I have always considered it to be a little beyond your capabilities as a hostess. Now can we leave it at that?"

Pig, I remember thinking.

Needless to say I couldn't remember the last time we had used it, most likely Christmas day.

"Did you get through your list today Marjorie?" George said. "I must be at the airport by 10.30am so you'll need to do the school run and then straight on. OK?"

"Yes, George, that's fine," I replied. "How long are you away for?"

"I'll be back on Sunday afternoon. But I won't be in long. I'm meeting a client in town in the evening so don't bother about dinner."

"Right, OK, that's fine," I said.

I looked across the table at the man I had married and wondered what the hell had gone wrong.

He's wasn't a bad man, I supposed. He didn't hit me or mistreat me. He provided for us and I didn't think he was deliberately cruel; he's just a different generation to me. He certainly could never be described as a new man, more an 18th Century 'women should be seen and not heard' man.

When we met, these proclivities were not immediately obvious. He just seemed mature and terribly sophisticated. It was as our relationship developed that I began to realise he veered to the far right of male chauvinism.

Fifteen years, I thought, and this is where we have got to.

I had met George at a conference in Blackpool. I had a successful career in sales, owned my own flat, had a company car and earned enough money to be comfortable. He was a good deal older than me and although not particularly good looking had a presence that always made him noticeable.

I got rather drunk one night and he very kindly escorted me back to my hotel room. Nondescript fumbling followed and phone numbers were exchanged. I played it cool believing him to be a love 'em and leave 'em type, and in truth I never expected to see him again. I was, however, wrong. He pursued me relentlessly.

He would send me flowers and presents or turn up on my doorstep with tickets to Paris for the weekend or train tickets to London to see a show.

It all seemed so romantic at the time. He was a real old fashioned man. Opening doors for me; ordering the wine when we went out for dinner. He even used to ask most politely if we could have sex. Compared to most of the men I had been out with he seemed like Mr Darcy personified.

An out and out charmer, I fell for him completely. I was totally in awe of his confidence and his success and one year later we were married. I was 31.

Even in the early days George was away a lot. His job meant he had to travel all over the world often at short notice. When we didn't have Rebecca and I still lived in the city it didn't bother me much. I would meet up with my friends and I still had my job.

However, when we found out I was pregnant George decided we should move to the country and that it would be better if I did not return to work.

Did I kick off about this? Did I rush out to the patio and burn my bra on his prize gas barbecue in protest? No, for my part I was quite happy to make the trade-off. I had a new husband, a new home and shortly after that a new baby.

I often used to wonder why George had been attracted to me. I realised years later, it was my child bearing hips. He would have considered me to be good breeding stock. Once I had produced, George went off and got the snip without even consulting me.

For years I loved being at home and looking after my child. It was where I absolutely wanted to be. Rebecca became my whole life, but with George away so much, I did find it lonely. I had lost touch with my old friends and seemed to have no success in making new ones. I ended up leading a very introverted and solitary life.

So what had my devotion and sacrifice earned me? The dubious honour of sitting round a table, with two people, that couldn't even be bothered to talk to me. Bloody marvellous!

After dinner we all went our separate ways, but not before Rebecca had checked that her Home Ec stuff was sorted.

"Did you get it all Mother?" she asked with an air of complete disinterest.

"Yes, I did," I said. "It's all together in a bag in the fridge. Funny one though, I had to make the Dulce…" I never got chance to finish.

"Yes, yes, all right. I don't need to know all the boring details do I? As long as it's all ready. I'm going up to my room now." She left the kitchen.

Ungrateful little cow, I fumed, and set about clearing up.

The next morning, I dutifully dropped Rebecca off at school and took George to the airport. On the drive back, I considered why I had started to feel so angry about things all the time. Surely I should be grateful for what I had, keep my mouth shut and my brain dead.

I could always leave I suppose, be brave and go it alone. Get a little house somewhere and go back to work. But I'd have to take Rebecca, could I seriously do that to her, turn her life upside down? She would have to leave her home, her school; she would hate me even more than she did already.

I was almost certain that George would never agree to a divorce, his sense of pride would never allow him to admit failure.

I was trapped. There was no way out, or at least not until Rebecca left home or went to University.

So what options did I have then? Therapy maybe? Perhaps someone could convince me that there was no reason to feel this way. That I was suffering from some kind of neurosis. After a couple of sessions and a bottle of pills I'd would be right as rain and seeing the world as wonderful again.

No, hang on, I knew people that had tried it. They all ended up madder than before. No – sometimes, ignorance absolutely is bliss. Looking too deeply into my dark inner thoughts was not a good idea.

There must be something I can do?

A little part time job perhaps? Surely no one could object to that. It wasn't as though I was needed at home as much now and it might just give me the sense of purpose I so desperately needed. George must be able to see that I'm not happy. He couldn't be either could he?

I decided I would broach the subject with him when I spoke to him that evening.

He rang on the dot at 7.30pm.

"Evening Marjorie," he said. "I trust all is well at the home-stead. Can I speak to Rebecca?"

"Yes, dear," I replied. "Everything is fine. I'll pass you over to Rebecca in a minute. There's something I have to talk to you about first, please."

"Really?" he sounded surprised. Admittedly, I could see why; our phone conversations were always brief.

"Yes, it's just, it's just..." I was trying so hard to find the right words.

"Come on woman spit it out," he grunted impatiently.

"I'd like to get a job, George," I blurted. "Nothing too time consuming, just something part-time. Being at home all day on my own, well, it's just not enough for me any more George. You don't mind do you?"

I was surprised by his reaction. He laughed. Not just a short laugh, but a long drawn out, loud, raucous laugh.

"Don't be so ridiculous woman!" he guffawed. "Who on earth is going to employ a 46 year old woman who's been out of the job market for 15 years? I mean, come on Marjorie what on earth would you be able to do? It's all computers these days and well, let's face it, your IT skills are pretty much non-existent. You can just about manage to surf your way round online grocery shopping and that's about it."

I was dumbfounded by his reaction. How dare this man make me feel so worthless?

"I could retrain," I retorted. "The local college offers all sorts of courses in IT."

"No, Marjorie absolutely not; you have a job: looking after me, Rebecca and the house."

I tried to protest, "But George it's just not enough any-more..."

"Look Marjorie!" I could hear he was starting to get an-noyed. "If you're short of spending money, I'll up your allowance."

"Oh, don't you see George? It's not about the money. It's about m..."

He interrupted me again.

"Enough Marjorie!" he was shouting, "Now please get Rebecca for me."

I put the phone down and called Rebecca with tears well-ing up in my eyes; partly because I was shocked at his reaction and partly because it felt as though my one small flicker of hope has been cruelly and brutally blown out.

I went into the kitchen and poured myself a very large glass of wine.

What was I supposed to do now? George had made it perfectly clear that returning to work was not approved of. I could do it anyway, I suppose. I mean things could hardly get any worse at home could they? Actually, yes , they probably could.

I considered my options and realised that I would have to stay put and brave it out?

But I can't stay as I am, I'll go mad or worse end up being so doped up on antidepressants I'd believe I was living in another world. Actually, that option does sound quite tempting. It would certainly save a hell of a lot of hassle.

No, I knew what I had to do. I needed to find my stiff upper lip, stop feeling sorry for myself, say sod it to everyone and within the realms of my little world endeavour to become a more fulfilled and interesting person.

I would get George to up my allowance, and use the extra to do things that would help me become happier. I hated the idea of taking more of his money, but what the hell, he had left me no choice. Finding one's self I suspected, would not come cheap.

2

Resurrected from the Dead

I decided that my first port of call in finding something to do should be the local library. Always a mine of information, I felt sure they would give me all the advice I would need.

Having got Rebecca on the school bus and with George still away, I drove the five miles or so to 'The Big Village' with renewed vigour and a real sense of excitement.

I didn't venture there very often, I found it too intimidating. The people were nosey and always wanted to know your business. I preferred the sanctuary and privacy of my home with its views of rolling hills and moorland.

I parked my car and noticed how nothing much had changed. The shops were all the same, but still it was prettier than I had remembered.

It had been years since I'd set foot in the library and I was amazed to find that it had been turned into a full blown community information centre with leaflets on all manner of things to do and places to go. I had begun pawing through some of the leaflets when an elderly lady approached me.

"Morning love, can I help you with anything?"

"I'm not sure," I said, sounding rather sheepish. "I'm looking for information on local groups and societies to join. Do you have that kind of information?"

"We most certainly do, dear, come over here and take a seat."

She gestured towards a desk and I dutifully sat on the chair beside it. She then bustled into the back and produced a large A4 binder which she plonked down with a thud.

"Have you just moved in round here then dear, or are you on holiday?"

"Err, no, I live here actually, well just down the road anyway. We've been here about 13 years."

She looked surprised. "Really dear, I thought I knew just about everybody round here. Whereabouts are you then?"

"We're in The Old Mill at Deering Falls."

She stopped and looked very puzzled. "Deering Falls, Deering Falls..."

I could see she was trying to remember something, then she blurted out,

"Oh my, that's where the Primm's live isn't it, I thought you looked vaguely familiar?"

I was taken aback by the fact that she knew who we were. "Yes, yes it is," I said enthusiastically. "I'm Marjorie Primm."

"Well, I'll be jiggered." She laughed a long and hearty laugh. "So you're Rebecca's mum then?"

I nodded.

"Well, well, I'll be blowed. We all thought you must be dead dear, that or you'd run off with the milkman." She dug her elbow playfully into my side and chortled.

I was puzzled. "I'm sorry, how do you mean?"

"Well, I mean you never come up to the village do you dear? We see your Rebecca in here all the time; bless her, but you dear, never. It's like you don't exist, Rebecca never talks about you, and well you know what villagers are like dear? What they don't know they makes up. They don't mean no harm, all a bit of fun really."

She carried on chortling in a manner I found quite disconcerting. My venturing into the library was obviously something of a revelation. I surmised that they either didn't get many people going in or that this very strange old lady was several sandwiches short of a picnic.

13

"Well, I'm glad I've been able to provide you with some light entertainment," I said, annoyed. "Now can you help me or not?"

"Now then, now then, let's not be getting all uppity. Have you time for a cuppa whilst you're looking. Nice cup of tea always helps focus the mind, I find. Don't you?"

It appeared that in my attempt to avoid the gossip and prying of village life I had in fact, made myself a target for it by not being seen. Clearly I had made the right move by deciding to get out more.

"I suppose so," I said. "Yes, thank you that would be very nice."

Humour her I decided, then make a break for the door!

"Right you are then, I'll be back in a jiffy."

She returned a few minutes later carrying a tray of tea.

"I'm Vera by the way," she said, handing me a large mug.

"Thank you, you're very kind."

"That's all right love, my pleasure. Now, let's have a look in this 'ere book shall we?

"Do you have any special interests, then, Marjorie?" She started looking through the pages. "Any hobbies, crafts you do, painting, drawing, peculiar sexual peccadilloes perhaps?"

I nearly choked on my tea. "Sorry?"

"Oh, just my little joke dear. Do you have any idea how boring it can be in here?"

This was one wacky old lady, I thought.

"No, No, I don't. I mean the drawing and painting, not the sex thing. Not that I have peculiar sexual tendencies either, I mean..." I was floundering.

She chortled away again. "It's alright love. I knew what you meant."

She glanced up when the chime went on the door. Thank God, I thought.

"Oh bother," she muttered. "Fred Emmerson's come in to change his books. The silly old bugger was only in yesterday; he'll 'ave forgotten most likely. Why don't you start looking through that and see what takes your fancy? I'll be back in a bit."

She went over to see to the gentleman that had just walked in.

I turned to the book and started to look through the hundreds of pages. Each one listed a different group or society that was within a ten mile radius of the village. I couldn't get over how many there were. My long held belief that village life was boring could not have been further from the truth.

Flower arranging, Field Society, pot holing, amateur dramatics, poetry groups, felting workshops, painting classes, dry stone walling, to name but a few. The subject array was mind boggling.

Vera came back. "Well any luck then?"

"There's so much to choose from," I said. "I haven't got a clue where to start."

"Well, you could just start at A and work your way through," she replied. "Oh, but that would mean you'd be straight in at Amateur Dramatics and I'm not sure you're ready for that one yet. Funny lot these luvvies."

"What would you recommend, Vera? What would you do in my shoes?"

"Well, if I'd just been resurrected from the dead I'd be tempted to join the Church choir," she chuckled.

"I don't think I can sing," I replied sarcastically.

She laughed, "Perhaps not then. I'd go for something easy and gentle to start with I think."

She paused and tapped her lip with her finger. "I know, what about flower arranging? That way, if someone decides you've died again, at least you can design your own wreath."

I laughed, but yes flower arranging, that sounded quite tame, almost relaxing.

"I think that's a great idea," I said enthusiastically.

"Marvellous, let me get you the details." She came back a few minutes later with a card that had the name and telephone number of the person I needed to contact.

"Now just you make sure you go young lady. I know several people that go to that class, and I'll soon know if you've bottled it."

"Young lady, Vera, come on I'm 46 years old for God's sake."

"Yes and I'm 89, so everyone's young compared to me. There's not much I haven't seen you know. Reckon I'm quite an expert on this human nature malarkey."

"Really," I said. "So what can you tell me about me then?"

"You, you dear, you've just woken up. You're just on the brink of taking a leap you never thought you'd take and this is your first step, but it won't be your last. This flower arranging thing, that's just the beginning you see. I can tell, you have that look about you."

"Look?" I said, "What look?" I felt as though I was in the middle of a Dickensian novel or some adventure by Robert Louis Stephenson. Was she about to slap the black spot on my forehead?

"The look of a woman who's lost her way and is trying to find it again."

My God – she's good, I thought. She's really, really good.

"Now go on, be off with you. You've taken up far too much of my very valuable time."

"Thank you Vera, thank you so very much. You have no idea how much help you've been."

"Oh, I do, dear, I do. Now go on."

I left the library and decided not to go straight back home. I felt somehow uplifted almost cheerful.

16

I wandered around the village looking at the shops. They were the usual touristy ones, but still they had some nice things.

I became aware of feeling guilty, as though recognising my own unhappiness was somehow a betrayal to George. That I was devaluing all he had done for me. I went into the chocolate shop and bought him some of his favourite chocolate Brazils.

Like a tourist, I carried on exploring the village. Looking at it afresh, it was quite beautiful. I noticed a new coffee shop on the corner and decided to treat myself. I ordered an extra-large cappuccino and a chocolate muffin and sat in the window watching the village I had feared so much go by.

I knew that if I went home and thought about it, I would talk myself out of making the call about the flower arranging, so I went back to the car and rang the number Vera had given me.

A very matronly posh voice answered the phone.

"Hello, Helena Duke speaking."

"Oh, hello Helena," my sheepish voice had returned, "I was given your number by Vera in the library. I'm ringing about joining your flower arranging classes."

"Who dear?" came the booming voice. "You'll have to speak up dear. I can't hear you."

"The flower arranging classes," I shouted. "Vera at the library said I should ring you."

"Oh, right, yes, I see. Well, we meet on a Thursday at 11.00am in the church hall on the high street. Do you have email dear? If you want to start this week, I'll need to send you the list of what you need?"

I flustered; email, email, did I have email? I couldn't remember.

"Err, I'm afraid I don't have one," I confessed.

"Don't have email, good grief woman, how on earth do you manage to survive? Oh well don't worry about it. I'll sort you something out and you can pay me for it on Thursday. But do try and get one as soon as you can; it makes life so much simpler."

"Yes, yes, I will thank you."

"Better take your name, dear, before you go, just so I know who to expect."

"It's Marjorie, Marjorie Primm," I said.

"Who dear, say again?"

"Marjorie, Marjorie, Primm!" I shouted.

There was a slight pause.

"Good God woman, we thought you were dead."

"No, no, an unfortunate mistake I'm afraid; I am very much alive," I shouted.

"That's one hell of a mistake, my dear. Oh well, no matter, we always welcome new members alive or dead. So can you make it this Thursday?"

I paused for a moment. Put on the spot my instinct was to say no, I'd think about it, but then I remembered Vera and what she had said. I took a deep breath.

"Yes, yes, I can make it."

"Jolly good," boomed the voice. "I'll look forward to meeting you."

"Yes, you too, bye."

I hung up and looked at my phone. I had done it, I had taken my first step in becoming a new person, and it felt great.

3

Wellingtons and Calla Lilies

Thursday arrived and I woke up feeling ridiculously nervous. George was still away, so all I had to deal with was getting Rebecca off to school.

We went through the usual silent routine that had become the breakfast ritual. Rebecca had her iPod firmly fixed into her ears so she didn't have to make conversation and I sat as usual with my cup of coffee staring out the window.

When I was younger, I had been a smoker, and I still missed that first cigarette of the day with my morning coffee. George had made it perfectly clear when we first met that smoking was not to be tolerated, so I did as I was told and gave up.

It was funny really, I hadn't realised before just how pliant I had allowed myself to become. How willing I had been to let this man I had once adored mould me, and change me in to something – somebody that I was never supposed to be.

In the early days he would go clothes shopping with me. I would try things on and he would say,

"No, dear, that's not you at all."

He would then go scour the rails for things he liked and tell me how lovely I looked in them, so I would say "OK" and wear them. Over the years I learned to pick out the clothes he liked automatically.

I'm not convinced George ever loved me for who I was, he loved me for what he thought I could become. I concluded that I was nothing more than a project, an unresolved disorganised jigsaw piece that had to be fitted neatly into his puzzle of life. Once he had accomplished this, I was just there, where I should be. No questions to be asked, no answers to be given.

I don't ever remember George asking me if I was happy. I don't ever remember him noticing if I was down, or us talking about anything beyond the day to day comings and goings of the house or Rebecca. I was convinced that when he was away, he simply believed we went into some kind of suspended animation. That our lives just went on hold until he came back.

I realised of course that this was not entirely George's fault. I had been quite willing to go along with it. I never protested or disagreed with him. I kept the status quo. After all, I was the one that had all the time; he was the one with the high pressured job. It was surely right that I supported him, becoming a nagging discontented wife was not the thing to do. Besides, I hated confrontation.

That, I concluded was the thought for the day. I was having a lot of those lately.

I finished my coffee and drove Rebecca to the pickup point for the school bus. I had two hours to kill before my venture into the unknown world of flower arranging.

What should I do?

Email, I would set up an email account. I signed onto the home computer and googled email accounts. Within five minutes I had a Hotmail account: joprimm49@hotmail.com

It was as simple as that.

I chose Jo because that's what I had always been known as at college. Marjorie was my Grandmother's name and I had always hated it. I remember when I got married my then best friend killing herself laughing saying,

"Marjorie Primm, my God, how far from the truth can you get?"

But I was Marjorie Primm; I had grown into my name. I had become the self-controlled, predictable, totally straight laced woman that my name suggested.

But no more, from now on I was Jo – Jo Primm. I liked it.

Feeling empowered I decided to further my explorations into the world of 'online' and proceeded to google Facebook.

Again within a few minutes I had a Facebook account. I didn't have a clue how it worked and decided to leave it alone until I returned from my class. I wasn't going to be late; I got the distinct impression that Helena Duke was not a woman to be messed with.

I arrived about ten minutes early and Helena was already there setting up.

There were half a dozen or so trestle tables set out with one placed at the front separate from the others. This was Helena's.

She looked exactly as her name and her voice would have implied, a mature lady with a large ample chest, tweed skirt and very sensible shoes. Definitely public school educated, definitely head girl and most certainly captain of the hockey team.

I lurked at the back of the room not sure what to do.

She was unwrapping flowers on the table and taking things out of bags. She looked up, glanced disparagingly at me and boomed, "Come in woman, come in! Don't loiter, you're either here or you're not."

I stepped forward.

"Hello, I said nervously, "I'm Marjorie Primm"

"Thought so," she said without glancing up. "Grab a table at the back, that way you can watch and learn as well as having a go."

I did as I was told and went and stood behind a table that was as close to hiding in the corner as possible. It felt like the first day of school again. I was scared, genuinely scared. This just didn't feel like it was going to be me at all.

Within a few minutes a troupe of about ten women all came chattering through the door. They were all laden down with bags and all laughing. I was surprised at the age range. It went from what seemed to be girls in their twenties right up to white haired old grannies. They all went to what were clearly their regular places and started to unpack their bags.

Several of them glanced over at me and smiled.

"Morning ladies," Helena said, "I hope you all have your flowers and apparatus as requested. Jean, I don't want you telling me again this week that you've forgotten your things."

"No Helena," shouted the voice next to me. "I got my arse into gear this week."

A laugh went round the room and I began to feel this could be a lot more fun than I had anticipated.

"Makes a change dear," Helena replied. "Now before we start ladies, we have a new class mate today. I'd like to introduce you all to Marjorie Primm." She gestured towards me at the back of the room.

I held my hand up and waved. "Hello," I said, "but please, call me Jo, not Marjorie."

"Hi Jo," came a chorus of voices.

"Right then." said Helena. "Shall we get started? As I told you last week we are attempting to push the boundaries of our flower arranging skills by making unexpected objects beautiful. Have you all got your wellington boots?"

"Yes Helena," sounded a chorus in reply.

"I've still got mine on," shouted one voice. "Didn't have time to change after milking, does it matter that it's still covered in cow shit?"

The room erupted into laughter again.

"I don't suppose it'll have to Beryl," said Helena. "Marjorie, sorry Jo, I'm lending you one of my old ones, you can let me have it back when it's done. She held out a green wellington and I went to the front of the class to collect it. She also handed me a bag with several Calla lilies, some oasis and various bits of green foliage in it.

I went back to my table.

"So ladies, let us begin. Let us make these wellington boots into things of beauty that we can place with pride in the halls of our homes."

Everyone began getting their flowers out of their bags. I stood confused, watching what everyone was doing. It was all a bit surreal; I'd imagined we would be making beautiful centre pieces for our dining tables not messing about with wellies. Jean leaned over to me.

"It's OK," she said with a smile "You just do what you think; there is no right or wrong way. Just go with the flow. She's quite a character our Helena, not what you expected, eh?"

"Err, no," I said.

Jean laughed, "It's the real reason we all keep coming back, to see what mad things she'll comes up with next. I've been coming for about five years now and she still keeps surprising me."

"Right," I said. "I see."

"Not everyone's cup of tea," she continued, "If you're into the more formal stuff there is another class in Home Bridge on a Friday."

"No, No," I said. "This is fine for me." And I kind of decided that it was. It was bizarrely appropriate that in my attempt to break my mould I should start with an alternative flower arranging class. It fitted perfectly.

"Helena," came a voice. "Mine keeps falling over. It won't stand up straight."

It belonged to one of the younger women of the group, a pretty girl dressed in a long print skirt and a bohemian style gypsy top.

"Now Caroline, what have I told you time and time again? Chicken wire is the florist's friend, it should be part of your tool kit in any arrangement you attempt. Have you got any?"

The girl shook her head.

"Well, you'll just have to borrow some of mine then, won't you?"

Helena went back to her table and brought out a piece of wire. She returned to Caroline and began stuffing it down her wellington boot.

"There you are dear, rigid as a groom on his wedding night. That's not going to go anywhere now is it?"

There was a roar of laughter from the entire room.

"Thanks for that Helena," said Caroline. "I'll never look at my wellies in the same way again."

As I struggled with my wellington boot, I watched and listened to the women around me. Beryl was a dairy farmer's wife, totally down to earth with a fabulous sense of humour; she had us all in stitches several times during the course of the class. Jean, I learned, was married to the local doctor and Caroline was married with a young son. She worked part time in the coffee shop I had been to a couple of days before.

"Right ladies," said Helena. "You have about five minutes to finish."

She began wandering round the room having a look at our work.

"Beryl dear, you were meant to be making something that could go in the house not something you could feed to the cows."

"What!" said Beryl indignantly. "It's rustic looking, that's all."

24

"Yes, dear, but there's rustic, and there's rustic. Keep trying dear, keep trying."

She finally reached my table.

"Not bad Jo, Not bad at all for a first attempt. Look everyone; see how she has used both form and height to balance out the height of the wellington."

"Bloody teacher's pet," laughed Beryl.

I had no idea what she was talking about, but it felt so good to be praised for something. I felt like a little kid that had got their homework right.

"Thank you, Helena," I said.

"Right ladies, next week we will be turning the humble frying pan into a wall garland. You can use any flowers you like, but Beryl that doesn't mean the cow parsley from the back of your barn."

"But I like cow parsley," beamed Beryl.

"I know, dear, but it does feature rather heavily in all your work. Push your boundaries Beryl, push your boundaries."

"Yes Helena," she said in a slightly dejected tone.

I had begun packing my things away when Jean and Beryl both came up to me.

"So what did you think?" said Beryl, "Wacky old bird isn't she?"

"Mildly eccentric," I smiled.

"That's one way of putting it," she replied. "That's quite a creation you've done there I could be almost jealous."

"I'm sorry," I said. "I didn't mean to, well, I hadn't meant to, to well tread on anyone's toes." I began to feel the old Marjorie returning.

"Don't be silly you daft cow, I'm pulling your leg. We just came over to tell you about our girls' night out. We do it once a month, just the local pubs nothing special. We all get together, get pissed and put the world to rights; the next one's a week on Friday if you fancy coming."

"Thanks, I'll see if I can make it," I said.

"Well, we'll remind you next week that is if you're daring to come back," said Jean with a grin.

"Oh I might just risk it," I laughed.

"OK then, we'll see you next week, bye."

"Bye."

We all pottered out into the early afternoon sunshine with our wellington boots for the entire world to see.

I had an overwhelming urge to show Vera my efforts so I went across the square to the library. I walked in and plonked my wellington boot in front of her on the desk.

"Ta dah," I laughed.

"Well now," she smiled. "Isn't that something?"

"I couldn't resist," I said. "I had to come and show you, don't quite know why, I hope you don't mind."

"Mind lovely, course I don't mind, I'm honoured you would think to. It's quite a work of art is that! Who'd of thought a humble wellie boot could look so, so..."

"Flowery."

"Yes, flowery, that's it. God love her, our Helena is truly a one off, isn't she?"

"She certainly is," I said.

"Well, I'm glad you had the guts to go love, you've got a beam on your face that says it all. But I'll ask anyway. Did you enjoy it?"

"Oh yes, Vera, yes I did, very much."

"So not the group of pitch fork wielding nosey parker villagers that you thought they'd be then, eh?"

"No, no, not at all; they were all lovely. Yes they asked questions, but nothing prying just simple things like where I lived, did I have any children, nothing scary or intimidating at all. I came away wishing it hadn't had to end. I've laughed more in the last hour and a half than I have in the last five years."

"Aye, they're a rum bunch those lasses, but hearts of gold you'll find. Cuppa?"

"Oh, yes please, Vera, if it's no trouble. I'm not keeping you from doing anything am I?"

"Not at all love, I think Fred Emmerson's in 'ere somewhere, but he'll find me if he needs me."

"He comes in here a lot doesn't he? Wasn't he here the other day when I first called in? He must be a really avid reader."

"Unfortunately not, dear, He's got Alzheimer's and can't remember if he's been in or not. God love him, takes out a different book each time he comes in but never brings it back. Quite often brings his own in by mistake. He thinks he loves to read, so whether or not he does I figures is neither here nor there as long as he's happy.

"I go to his house once a week to pick up the ones he's forgotten and take back the ones he's brought in by mistake. We 'as a nice cup of tea and he tells me his woes. Just bloody thankful I still has all me marbles I can tell ya, or wells most of 'em anyway."

She chuckled and pottered off to the kitchen and presently came back with a tray of tea and biscuits.

"Well, I'm so glad you enjoyed the class, I thought that might be a good one for you to start with. There is a more formal one you could have gone to, but I kind of figured you might have had enough of being formal. This is, how can I say it nicely, more avant-garde. Yes, that's it."

She poured the tea.

"Well, I have to confess," I said. "It was not at all what I had expected. I'd imagined it to be Stepford type wives making centre pieces for their frightfully posh dinner parties.

But it wasn't, they made me feel so welcome. They were all so at ease with themselves, so comfortable in their own skins. Each one was warm, funny and friendly and most surprising of all, totally accepting of me."

Vera laughed, "Well, why wouldn't they be, you silly mare, it's not like you've got two heads now is it? Actually, thinking about it, that's not such a good example to give round here, all the interbreeding that's gone on that is more than possible," she chuckled.

"They even invited me on a night out in a couple of weeks. I couldn't believe it, they hardly know me. I can't go, of course, but, it was so lovely just to be asked. I can't remember the last time I got invited to anything."

"Why can't you go?"

"Oh, well George is away so much and even if he was at home, he would never agree to babysit so I could have a night out. My god I can just imagine his reaction."

"Marjorie, If I had meant you to go out I would not have fitted you with a z-wave activated combination chastity belt now would I?" I laughed. "No, unfortunately it just isn't an option."

"You, my girl, need a bloody good kick up the backside. You jolly well find out if that bugger of a husband of yours is about that Friday and you jolly well tell him you're going. If you gets any arguments just tell him you can't babysit your own child, or better still bloody well send 'im to me."

She genuinely was quite angry about it.

"Oh, I don't think so Vera, I'm not sure I can cope with the aggravation that it would all cause."

"Now you listen here Marjorie Primm, you can't give up now. You're on the brink of claiming back your life and I for one am not going to let you give up. You give way on this small thing and you might as well just resign yourself to the

Valium and a bottle of gin a week for the rest of your life. Is that all you think you're worth?"

The passion of her words was almost evangelical.

"Oh, come on Vera, missing one night out is hardly giving up is it?" I said glibly.

"OK," she said. "Tell me this then. When you were asked by the girls if you wanted to go on their night out, what was your reaction, your first gut reaction?"

I thought about it for a moment.

"I thought yes, yes, I'd love to," I said.

"But then you started thinking about George and home and the logistics and the fact that he wouldn't like it and told yourself no, right?"

"Well, yes," I said.

"Don't you see Jo, George is always going to say no to everything you want to do? By not going on your girls' night out you're just postponing what will still be an inevitable argument about something you want to do that he doesn't think you should. Don't you get it? He's controlling you. Heaven knows why he needs to, but he thinks he does, and the longer you lets him the harder it'll be. Do you want to just carry on the way you were? Or does that sad pathetic creature that came into the library the other day, want to break free?"

I couldn't get over how impassioned she was about this; something told me that for some reason my particular circumstances had touched a nerve.

Had she once been like me, perhaps?

"I'm just not sure I'm ready Vera," I said anxiously.

"Oh, don't be so ridiculous woman, he doesn't hit you does he?"

"No, no of course not," I said reassuringly.

"Well then, my guess would be that the worst you can expect is a display of extreme sulking and in my experience that as often as not is usually quite amusing."

"Do you think so?" I said doubtfully.

"I do," she said resolutely. "Just do it Jo, make it happen. I promise you, you'll be amazed at how good it'll feel."

"OK," I said confidently, "I'll give it a go, but I'm not promising anything."

"That's my girl, cheers." She clanked her tea cup against mine.

"Well, I'd better be going," I said. "Thanks for the tea and the pep talk Vera."

I stood up and went round the back of the desk and gave her a hug. I wasn't prone to hugging. It was a habit that over the years I had weaned myself off. But now in the company of this lovely forthright woman, it seemed the very least I could do at that moment to show her that I appreciated her words.

I took my wellie and walked back to the car. I placed it very carefully in the boot with a rug gently folded around its base to hold it firm and set off on the drive home, reflecting on the morning's events.

The sun was shining and the hills that had seemed so depressing a few days before now seemed lush and full of life. I passed a field of grazing Friesians and contemplated how idyllic it all was. I was feeling quite lyrical; cows I thought, such soft creatures with breath like….

"Shit, I knew there was something I'd forgotten. We need milk."

I turned round and went to one of the few local shops between the village and home. I got the milk and placed it on the counter, then without consciously registering what I had done, asked for ten cigarettes as well.

I got back in the car and smuggled them immediately into my handbag, fearing someone might have seen my act of purchasing contraband. I decided I was safe, the only people around were a couple snogging on the bench by the river, and they were far too engrossed in how far their tongues could get down each other's throats to notice me.

I got home, made myself a coffee and went out into the garden. I took the cigarettes out of my bag. Why had I bought them, I wondered? Why, after so many years, had I impulse purchased these dreadful things, a subconscious act of defiance perhaps? I undid the packet, took one out and lit it. It made me light headed and I felt a bit sick, but I persevered.

It felt naughty and ever so slightly dangerous, just like the bike sheds at school or the balcony of my flat before George would come round. I had a constant supply of breath fresheners tucked down my top in those days.

I decided this would be my controlled rebellion; I would have a very occasional cigarette that no one knew about. It would be my secret pleasure.

I finished my coffee and went back into the house.

I seemed to complete the tasks of the day with renewed energy and by the time Rebecca got home all was as it should be.

I made dinner and Rebecca made her usual excuses to go and do her homework, I knew I wouldn't see her again until she came down to say goodnight.

As she was going through the hall, she suddenly came back into the kitchen looking baffled.

"Mother!" she exclaimed. "There's a wellington boot on the hall table with a load of flowers in it."

"Yes, dear," I said. "There is."

"Why?" she said, puzzled.

"Why not?" I replied.

4

Am-Dram or Jerusalem

Friday morning brought two unexpected events. A phone call from George to say he would be home on Sunday morning for approximately a week, and an actual conversation with Rebecca over the breakfast table. A leaflet had gone round her drama group at school asking for people to come and audition for the village panto.

"Please can I go Mum? I know loads of people that are doing it, it's on Sunday afternoon at 2.00pm."

"I don't' see why not hun," I said. "Do you want me to come with you?"

"Well, I could do with a lift there, I don't think it will take that long, apparently if you turn up you're pretty much guaranteed a part, even if it's only in the chorus."

"OK then," I said. "If it's something you really want to have a go at."

I drove her to the bus stop and returned home. The idea of George coming home did not fill me with excitement, quite the opposite. I had got so used to him being away all the time that I usually found his return visits intrusive. However, if he was around on the Friday, I might be able to persuade him to let me go on the girls' night out. I was still caught up in thoughts about my flower arranging class and couldn't help chuckling every time I went past the wellington boot in the hallway. That cheered me up a bit.

My next task was to have a go at the Facebook thing. I logged on to my account and had a good look through the instructions. I began trying to remember the names of all the people I had known at college and work, trouble was a lot of them would be married now and I didn't know their surnames.

After about an hour, I decided it was a pointless exercise and went and made myself a coffee and had my secret cigarette behind the greenhouse.

The rest of the weekend was uneventful; Rebecca was away at a friend's on the Friday night so I lost the evening watching stupid girlie films. I never could understand why I had the propensity to do this. Every time someone said I love you or made a romantic gesture, I hurled verbal abuse at the screen. I was an out and out cynic when it came to matters of the heart.

On the Saturday, Rebecca and I went to town to have our hair cut. The banter in the hairdressers was the same old stuff, woman moaning about their weight, their looks, their husbands or partners. It all seemed so trite.

I was almost tempted to try something different, but chickened out and had my usual trim. Maybe next time, I told myself.

We followed the excitement of the hairdressers with an equally exciting trip to the supermarket. I didn't have a clue where anything was and after ten minutes of trying to negotiate a wonky wheeled trolley round people standing in the middle of isles chatting, I decided that including a weekly shopping trip into my list of adventurous things to do was not an option. Online shopping for groceries was definitely preferred.

Rebecca had asked if she could have her friend Millie over for a sleepover and in my effort to be more sociable, I said yes, so we picked her up on the way back from town.

They had a very noisy, but I think fun time and it was nice to hear Rebecca laughing so much for a change.

Sunday came and it was time for 'the big audition'. It turned out Millie was going for it too, so I rang her parents and said she could come along with us and they agreed they would pick her up afterwards.

The meeting was at the Town Hall quite an impressive set up for such a small place. It had a proper decent sized stage and seated about 250 people. I had been there once or twice in the past in the days when George and I used to venture out together, but not recently.

I was surprised at how many people were there. It looked like about 40 or so and the noise was deafening. I felt out of my depth. Rebecca on the other hand was straight in there and she and Millie immediately found a group of their friends from school and I found myself abandoned.

I was just about to leave and go sit in the car when a rather distinguished looking gentleman came over to me.

"Rowdy bunch aren't they?" he said.

"It is rather noisy," I replied.

"Have you come to audition?" he said.

"Me, good God no; I've brought my daughter, she wants a part."

"Well, you should think about it," he said. "We always need adult members you know, even if you just wanted to be in the chorus."

"I can't sing or dance," I said.

"Perfect," he smiled. "Nor can any of the others. Think about it." He wandered off to talk to someone else.

I pondered on what he had said. I wasn't aware that I had ever had aspirations to go on the stage. But I suppose it would be another way of meeting people and it would be rather nice to be involved in something Rebecca and I could do together.

My thoughts were broken by a rather formidable woman shouting for everyone to be quiet. She was a little older than me, tall with a long shock of white hair, dressed head to foot in what I could only describe as floaty stuff.

"Hello everybody!" she bellowed. "How simply marvellous to see so many of you here."

My thoughts immediately jumped to what Vera had said about luvvies that day, in the library, and I smiled to myself. Yep, I think I had just had my first sighting.

She continued. "Now if you could all find a chair and sit down we will start the auditions. For those of you that don't know, this year we are doing Cinderella." She waved her arms in a swooping open gesture on the word Cinderella.

"If you're happy to just be in the chorus, please go over and see Alison, she will take your name and telephone number, then if you wish you may go."

Rebecca came and found me.

"Mum, what should I do, I don't know whether to go for a part or not?"

"It's up to you sweetheart," I said. "If you didn't get one would you still be happy just being in the chorus?"

"Hmm..." she puzzled. "I suppose it depends if any of my friends get parts and I don't."

I put my arm around her shoulders and gave her a squeeze. "Well, why don't you give it your best shot and just see what happens?"

"Oh, OK, I will. Thanks Mum."

She started off to go back to her friends.

"Rebecca," I called after her. "How would you feel about me being in the chorus?"

She looked horrified. "You Mum, why on earth would you want to do that?"

"Well, you're the one that's always telling me I should do more," I said.

"Well, yeah, I know, but this, is it really your kind of thing do you think?"

"Well, I won't know unless I try will I?" I said. "The point is would it bother you, I don't want to cramp your style or anything?"

She laughed. "Hell no, go for it Mum."

I went and put my name down on the list, then went and sat at the back to wait for Rebecca.

The auditions began and I watched with great interest the varied array of people that went up for parts. They truly were a mixed bag. Some were amazingly good and some were absolutely atrocious. The rather nice gentleman I had met earlier came back over and sat next to me.

"I saw you took the plunge," he smiled. "Good for you."

"Well, we'll see," I said. "I'm not promising that I'll stick at it, I've never done anything like this before."

"Oh, you'll be amazed," he said. "It gets under your skin this am-dram thing; they are a good bunch once you get to know them. Don't be put off by the OTT ones, there are far more of us that are sane than not."

"I'm Ian Henderson by the way." He held out his hand.

"Jo Primm," I shook his hand. "Pleased to meet you."

He then very kindly filled me in on who was who, and what was what.

Turned out he was on the committee and was one of the main protagonists of the group. I found this rather reassuring as he was obviously great fun but by no means the epitome of a 'luvvy'.

The formidable floaty lady was Imelda Falthrop, the director. Apparently, she had previously had some small success on the professional stage when she was younger as a dancer. She now had more of a reputation for stealing other people's husbands, a very flexible woman for her age, I was given to understand.

Jean from the flower club's husband, the doctor, was also involved. As was Jean herself; but she didn't go on stage as she apparently always helped with props and costumes.

I sat and waited patiently until it was Rebecca's turn to read. I was full of admiration that she had dared to go for the part of Cinderella. She did amazingly well, but even I could see that the role was destined for an older girl that had also had some professional training. I felt sorry for Rebecca, but at least she'd had the courage to go for it. More than could have ever been said of me.

The auditions plodded on. It seemed everyone that had come along that afternoon had aspirations to be in the main cast.

Ian was an absolute gem and seemed to sense my fear of the unknown. He went out of his way to keep introducing me to people so that by the end of the afternoon I felt like a veritable socialite.

We finally left the hall at 6.00pm being told that anyone who had a part would be rung over the next couple of days.

It was lovely driving back in the car. Rebecca was so excited about being in the show and for once we had something we could both talk about.

I had for the second time that week made some new friends and I felt real progress in my quest to be more visible.

As we pulled up the drive, I saw George's car. I had completely forgotten he was coming home.

We got in and found him in the living room reading the paper. Rebecca went rushing over to give him a big hug, and plonked herself on his lap.

"Daddy, Daddy, you'll never guess what we've been doing this afternoon!" she enthused.

"I couldn't possibly imagine kitten," he replied. "I thought you'd both left home when I got back and found the house empty."

"Sorry George," I said. "I should have left a note, I hadn't realised how long we would be out."

"We've been to audition for the panto Dad, I read to be Cinderella. Mum said she thought I was ever so good and Mum's signed up to be in the chorus."

"Really, Marjorie is that right, you're surely not being serious?" he said disapprovingly.

"Quite serious George, I thought it was about time I got out a bit more."

"I see." He paused.

"Well, I can understand Rebecca wanting to do something like that at her age, but for you, I don't think so dear. If you want to get out more, why don't you join the WI or something?"

I had a feeling he would react like this, typical of George. He hated anything that could potentially disrupt his sense of order and command.

"I don't honestly think it will affect you George. They rehearse twice a week and I'll have to go to take Rebecca along anyway."

"Still, not sure I'm happy to have my wife prancing about on a stage, it's hardly respectable is it?" he said disparagingly.

I started to feel quite annoyed; he'd been back in the house all of five minutes and was already telling me what I could and couldn't do.

"I suppose I could join the WI," I said. "Could be a lot more interesting than panto, although I'm not sure how I would feel about taking my clothes off."

"What! What are you talking about woman?"

"Oh, surely you haven't forgotten George, the WI round here are rather partial to going *au naturel*? All for a very good cause, of course, so I suppose I would have to consider it. Panto on the other hand, I am assured has never been known for its nude chorus numbers; would probably get better houses if it was. Let me know which you would prefer." I left the room.

I prepared dinner and George and I maintained a quiet standoff. Rebecca thankfully was oblivious, she chatted to her dad about what she had been doing whilst he was away and in fairness George was attentive and genuinely interested in what she had to say.

Rebecca then went off to bed and George and I were left alone.

"By the way," he said. "I found a wellington boot on the hall table with some flowers in it. I assumed you had left it there by mistake, so I've put it by the greenhouse."

My God, the flower arrangement, I should have known he'd hate it.

"Actually, George, it was meant to be there," I said. "That was the other thing, I was going to tell you about, I've started going to a flower arranging class. That was my first assignment. The teacher said she thought it was rather good."

"Really!" he said, sounding surprised. "Well, I'm sorry dear but I think I would have to question the qualifications of your teacher. Who ever heard of putting a flower arrangement in a wellington? Quite ridiculous."

My heart sank and I felt utterly dejected. Everything I had done over the last week had been rejected and scorned. It felt as though all the effort I had made was for nothing. I went into the kitchen and made myself a coffee.

"Get me a brandy whilst you're in there, will you Marj?"

Bastard, I'll give you brandy and I know just where I want to stick it.

I was quite taken aback by the feeling of my own anger. He has no idea what he's doing. He unequivocally is an insensitive pig.

I looked out of the window to be confronted by my own reflection. A sad, hopeless looking face stared back at me. I looked old, tired and forlorn. It was ridiculous to think that after all this time I could have expected him to realise why I had to change. Perhaps I should just forget it all and go back to being good old dependable Marjorie.

No, I resolved. Not this time. I will not let this man make me feel worthless any more. I am going to stick to my guns and I am going to see these things I have started through.

I took him his brandy.

"I'm going up now George, so I'll see you in the morning. Oh, but one last thing, are you about on Friday night?"

"As far as I know I am," he said.

"Good," I said, as I went up the stairs. "Because I'm going on a girls' night out and I need you to be here to look after Rebecca."

He didn't even get chance to reply, by the time I'd finished the sentence I was safely in my room with the door shut.

5
Champagne and Lingerie

The week that followed was fraught. George had obviously taken umbrage to my new-found self and spent the whole time shut up in his study barking for tea and snacks. Not that this was noticeably any different from his normal routine; there was just a little more grunting to contend with.

The up side was that the effort I had made the previous week with Rebecca was paying off and she had started to have limited conversations with me. We had received the call from the panto committee and although she hadn't got the part of Cinderella, she had been given a part as a page as well as being in the chorus. She had a few lines, which she seemed to be content with.

The other rather nice thing was getting 25 new friend requests on Facebook as a result of going to the auditions.

Thursday arrived and I went to my flower arranging class armed with an old frying pan a mixed bunch of flowers and of course the obligatory chicken wire.

The class was as much fun as the previous week and I was once again complimented on my arrangement.

I didn't care what George thought any more, it would be hung in the kitchen, whether he liked it or not. Besides, he never went in there anyway.

I talked to the girls about the arrangements for the Friday night and Beryl very kindly offered me a bed at hers if I decided I wanted to have a drink. I thanked her but said I didn't think so; I had better make sure I went home.

After dinner George once again ensconced himself in his study and I set about doing my usual chores.

I was still trying to catch up on all the laundry he had brought back with him and decided I would put a wash on so I could get it out and drying early the next morning.

I started going through his pockets, more out of habit than anything else, he was very good at making sure he never left anything in them so it was rather a surprise when I found a small wodge of receipts stuffed in the back pocket of a pair of trousers.

I took them out and just plonked them on the top of the washer. I glanced up after I had stuffed the clothes into the machine and the top of one of the receipts caught my eye.

La Senza it said. The name rang a bell. I unfurled it further and read on: Removable Push Up Babydoll £45.00, Ruched Merry widow £35.00, Costume Lace up Bustier £35.00, Luxe Classic Suspender with Lace £15.00.

I hurriedly scanned it further. I found the store location was Leeds and the date 15th June that was last Friday.

I stupidly asked myself the question, "Why on earth is George buying lingerie and why hasn't he given me it yet?"

I unfurled the other receipt it was an A4 hotel bill from Malmaison also in Leeds, dated 17th June, the Sunday he came home. It read: *Two night stay. Room charge £160.00 per night. Restaurant bill £195.00, Champagne and flowers on arrival to room £130.00.*

I was puzzled. So he came back into the country on Friday. Why did he stay in Leeds, why didn't he just come straight back home?

It's amazing how thick you can be when faced with two very obvious things, it genuinely took several minutes for the penny to drop.

When it finally did, I was stunned. I couldn't move, I just kept reading the receipts over and over again. I somehow felt if I kept looking at them, the writing would change and I would find I had made a mistake; that my brain would come up with a rational explanation and I would be able to forget I had ever seen them.

I must have stood there for over 20 minutes, thoughts racing through my head. He was having an affair; the low life arse hole was having an affair, how dare he? My immediate instinct was to march straight into his study and confront him.

I hesitated. "Hang on a minute Jo," I said to myself. "Don't do anything rash, go into the kitchen, pour yourself a stiff drink and think this through."

I made myself a very large gin and tonic and sat in the rocking chair by the Aga. There was something very comforting about an Aga, it was a calm, warm space that had associations of homely cosiness. It was my safe place.

I pondered over the idea of George being unfaithful. Was it genuinely such a shock? The more I thought about it the more I decided it wasn't shocking at all.

After all our sex life was non-existent. I couldn't remember the last time we'd '*done it*' and even in the days when we did, sex with George was never the most memorable of events. He was strictly a straight down to business kind of man. I used to find it quite boring and was always so pleased that it never seemed to last too long.

It took me a while to come to the conclusion that it was well before we'd moved into separate bedrooms. That was at least five years ago.

I then thought about the lingerie purchases for his mistress, he'd never, ever bought me lingerie. The whole thing of the hotel and the champagne conjured up a picture of sexy frolicking and fun that I just could not see George doing. But clearly he had.

I turned my thoughts to myself and began to wonder if it was my fault.

It's fair to say sex had always been a hard topic for me to talk about. I'd had a couple of fairly short lived relationships before I met George so my experience was pretty limited.

All my sexual encounters, including George, led me to believe that sex was very much for the benefit of the man and that a woman's role was to lay back and fake orgasm at the appropriate moment.

I laughed to myself. Perhaps joining the am-dram set was the right thing to do after all, my acting skills in that particular department were par excellence. Thank God for films otherwise I wouldn't have had a clue.

As a result of these mediocre experiences my libido was now non-existent. Sex never even crossed my mind, although to be fair to myself even if I did get the urge I'm not entirely sure I would recognise what it was. I did not consider myself to be attractive and I certainly wasn't sexy. It just didn't feature on my radar at all. It was however still very much featured on George's. Perhaps it wasn't such a bad thing that he was getting his carnal pleasures elsewhere. I started feeling sorry for him, he clearly felt I wasn't able to give him what he wanted or needed.

I began to wonder how long this affair had been going on. Had it just happened or had he been at it for years? Was it the same woman each time or did he have a string of lovers that he entertained? More worryingly was he suddenly going to blurt out one morning over his toast and marmalade that he was leaving me?

His behavior hadn't been noticeably different over the last few months, but then again would I have noticed? I had been so pre-occupied with my own troubles.

I began to feel scared.

No, keep calm. He's still coming home and he's still supporting me and Rebecca. Whatever he thinks of our relationship, he would never do anything to upset her life. For all his faults, he's a good dad and he loves his daughter.

Perhaps, he's like me then, he's just holding it all together until she's independent. I honestly didn't know. I decided that for now, though, I would keep quiet and say nothing.

I went and knocked on the study door.

"George, I'm off to bed now. Can I get you anything before I go up?"

"No, thank you Marj, I'm fine." He barely even registered my presence.

"OK then," I said. "You haven't forgotten about tomorrow night have you?"

"No," he said in a sarcastic tone. "Although I don't see why I should have to babysit whilst you go gadding about."

Here we go, I thought.

"George," I said firmly. "You can't babysit your own child, it's called being a parent and it's not like I ask you all the time."

"Well, I'm not happy about it," he said. "Not happy at all."

I was so tempted to say, "No and I'm not happy that you're cavorting with some little tart in Leeds in your spare time either, but there you go."

But I didn't. Instead I said,

"Oh well if you're already annoyed, I might as well go the whole hog and take Beryl up on her offer. I'm going to stay at hers tomorrow night. OK?"

I slammed the study door behind me.

"Marjorie, Marjorie, you're just being ridiculous!" George shouted after me.

I ignored him and went to bed.

He wasn't speaking to me at breakfast. I'm not sure if he was angry or just totally confused.

I wondered if I was being fair to him by not letting on that I knew what he had been up to. Perhaps thrashing it out was the right thing to do.

Did I want to cause that amount of upset though? It's not like I had passionate designs on him. I had decided that I didn't care that he was having sex with someone else. If my life was destined to be different it would me that made it so, not some other woman.

The day dragged on. George and I kept out of each other's way as much as possible and I finally went upstairs to get ready.

I was due to meet the girls at 7.30pm. I couldn't understand why, but I was ridiculously excited at the prospect of going out. The day's standoff with George had made me feel defiant and feisty and I was determined to make the most of my night of freedom. It was as though the knowledge I now had gave me some kind of power. George's indiscretions had broken the rules of the game and there were no limits anymore. Anything was possible.

I gave myself plenty of time to get ready choosing what to wear with care, it had been so long since I had done anything like this, I had no idea what to go for. In the end, I settled for smart casual and decided I would even put on makeup.

In the shower, I contemplated why George had given up on me physically. Was I that unattractive, so undesirable? After all, he hadn't put up much of a fight to maintain our sex life. Was it really all down to me? Was I so boring in bed that I just wasn't worth the effort? Perhaps I was getting what I deserved.

I couldn't get this train of thought out of my head so whilst I was getting dry I took a long hard look at my naked body. I studied myself carefully. Yes, I had put on a few pounds and there was certainly a good amount of cellulite visible, but my boobs were still in pretty good shape. It wasn't a perfect body by any means, but nor was it hideous. Monday morning I decided, I will go and join the gym. A bit of firming up is required.

I finished getting dressed and glanced in the mirror again. I decided that provided I kept out of bright lights I might just get away with being OK. I went downstairs.

"I'm off now George," I shouted.

No reply.

Rebecca came bubbling out the living room.

"Oh Mummy you look so pretty," she said.

"Thank you, sweetheart," I said. "What a nice thing to say. Where's your father?"

"He's in there," she gestured to the living room. "He's sulking, but don't worry, I'm going to make him sit and watch a DVD with me. You go out and have a lovely time." She reached over and gave me a kiss on the cheek.

"Are you sure you'll be all right?" I said.

"We'll be fine, now go on," she smiled.

"OK, well, I will be back in the morning, any problems give me a call on my mobile, this is Beryl's number if you need it." I handed her a piece of paper and gave her a hug and a kiss.

I tried once more with George.

"Bye then," I shouted.

No reply.

I left the house feeling a little nervous and drove to the village.

6

White Wine and Soft Kisses

Beryl had said I could drop my stuff off at her house and leave the car there. Her husband Bill, had kindly offered to run us down to the pub and pick us up when we were ready to come home.

I tried to remember the last time I had stayed away, I couldn't. Was I brave enough to go through with this? Not only was I going to the pub for the evening, but I was staying out all night as well. I had a sudden unexpected pang of conscience; this was no way for a mature woman to behave. George was right, I shouldn't be gadding about; I should be at home with my family.

A sudden tap on the car window broke my train of thought and startled me.

A tall, rugged and rather handsome man I'd guess was in his fifties, stood at the side of the car. I wound the window down.

"Eh up love, ya looked like a scared rabbit then, you OK?"

"Err, yes. Yes, thank you, I'm fine," I stammered. "I'm Jo, I'm meant to be going out with Beryl tonight."

"Ah, so you're Jo. Well, it's nice to meet you love, I'm Bill, Beryl's long suffering." He smiled, a lovely open and genuine smile.

I laughed. "It's nice to meet you too. It is kind of you to let me stay over; I hope it's not too much of an inconvenience." I got out of the car.

"Ha," he grinned. "Not at all, our house is always full of folks, she likes her mates over does our Beryl. I'm just glad

I've got me barn to go hide in when they all gets a bit frisky."
He winked.

I went to get my bag out the boot.

"I'll get that for you love." He reached over and took it from me. "Bloody hell, what you got in here your husband's body? I thought you were only stopping a night."

"Oh gosh, I'm sorry, shall I carry it?"

"I'm joking ya daft bint, now come on, Beryl 'al be accusing me of chatting you up if we don't get inside."

I followed him into the farmhouse.

The door led straight into a lovely, very large, warm, cosy, kitchen. The low beamed ceiling had all sorts of herbs, old pots and copper pans hanging from it and in the middle was a huge pine table and chairs. The sideboard was adorned with photographs taken of her two boys at various ages. The boys, I had learned from flower class, were both now living away, one was at college and the other university and Beryl missed them terribly. I felt a faint pang of jealousy at how happy they all looked.

"Right," said Bill, rubbing his hands. "Old bag's still upstairs getting ready. Why don't you have a seat and I'll get you a drink?"

I pulled out a chair and sat at the kitchen table. In pride of place on the middle of it was Beryl's wellington boot. I smiled.

Bill saw me looking at it. "Bloody bonkers that Helena," he laughed. "But Beryl loves going, I just have to put my lying head on every time she comes home with some new creation. Bless her; she's no flower arranger our lass, but I'd hate to hurt her feelings when she tries so hard."

What a lovely man, I wonder if Beryl realises how lucky she is.

"So what's your poison, then?" he said.

"Oh gosh, what have you got?"

"Well, we opened a rather nice bottle of home-made rhubarb wine at tea; if you're feeling brave you can have a glass of that?"

"I've never had home-made wine, sounds rather lovely. Yes, please."

He poured two glasses of cloudy looking wine and handed one to me.

"Cheers." We clinked and I took a sip.

I was surprised at how nice it was, quite tart, but surprisingly smooth a bit like a very dry Sauvignon Blanc.

"I'll go give Beryl a shout," he said. "Let her know you're here." He disappeared out of a door at the far end of the kitchen.

I took several more sips of my wine; it was starting to give me a rather nice warm feeling inside.

A few minutes later, Beryl came bouncing into the room.

"Jo!" She came over and gave me a big hug. "How lovely to see you. God you scrub up well don't you? It doesn't seem to matter how long I spend trying, I still end up looking as though I've spent the day with my head up a cow's arse."

"Thanks," I said. "But you look pretty good to me."

Bill came back into the room. "And to me." He went up behind her and gave her bum a cheeky pat. Then wrapped his arms around her waist and plonked a big kiss on her neck.

"Aye you, keep your hands to yourself, we've got company. You be on your best behaviour." She smacked his hands away laughing.

"Spoilsport." He laughed and came and sat at the table.

"So what you both drinking?" she asked, then saw the bottle on the table.

"Christ Bill, you've not let her loose on the rhubarb have you, she'll be pissed before we even get to the pub!" She lifted the bottle to see how much was left.

"Phew, still a fair bit's left, bloody lethal brew our rhubarb, strictly for professional drinkers. I'd make that your only glass if I were you Jo."

"Oh, I don't know, I said. "It's rather nice, it's making me feel all warm and relaxed."

"Yeah, well trust me, don't have any more, otherwise I won't be held responsible for your actions."

We carried on chatting and despite my urge to have more, I stuck to the one glass of rhubarb. Apparently home-made wine can be a lot more potent than normal.

I found myself fascinated by Bill and Beryl's interaction. I couldn't get over how different their relationship was to mine and George's. They clearly loved each other very much. My pang of jealousy returned and I felt overwhelmingly sad.

We finished our drinks and Bill drove us down to the village in his Land Rover, the three of us squished together on the front seat.

It smelled of hay and cows and reminded me of the holidays I had with my family as a child staying in a cottage on a farm in the Lake District. We walked, explored and spent loads of time just helping out on the farm. I remember sitting on top of wagons piled high with bales after hay making and thinking it was the most exciting thing ever. Simple, uncomplicated holidays, not the kind of thing that kids would buy into today.

We pulled up outside the pub and both scrambled out. Beryl went round to Bill's window, leaned in and gave him a big kiss.

"I'll ring you when we're ready to come home," she said softly.

"Now you two, just take it steady tonight, I know what you girlies are like when you've had a few," he scorned jokingly.

"Oh, be off with you, ya boring old bugger, go play doms with your old cronies." She waved him away. He laughed and drove off waving his arm out the window.

"Right," she said, winking at me. "Here we go!" She linked her arm through mine and we walked into the pub. Jean, Caroline and Caroline's mum Barbara, who was up for the weekend from Leeds, were already there and a rowdy cheer went up as we walked in.

"You're late!" said Jean. "You're at least two rounds behind, get to the bar ya slackers."

The pub was loud and full. Even in the middle of the country Friday night was still the usual end of the week celebration, same as I remembered from when I lived in the city. God, I reminisced, I always used to go out for a drink at the weekend, I was once upon a time a social creature. We bought the drinks and sat down.

I had decided to stick with white wine in view of my already having the rhubarb at Beryl's. It was going down surprisingly well, even though I wasn't much of a drinker. There had been a time when I had tried comforting my loneliness by downing a few glasses of wine, it just made me more depressed. It was a slippery slope that I declined, besides, there was no fun in drinking on your own; that was just sad.

The conversation and the wine flowed freely and I think it would be fair to say by my fourth glass I was well on my way. I had forgotten how silly I was when I was drunk. Some people get morose, some become loud and belligerent. Me, I just get happy.

As with all alcohol fuelled girls' nights out the conversation went from the mundane to the spice of life and the subject of sex came up. It was a comment that Beryl made that got us talking about it. Something about having to keep on the conscious side of drunk otherwise Bill wouldn't get his usual Friday night leg over, and that apparently would never do.

"I have a confession to make," said Caroline looking coy.

A gaggle of voices begged her to continue.

"Well, you know I told you I'd gone off sex a bit after having Matthew. More through tiredness than anything I think. Well, Andrew thought he might get me back on the horse again, so to speak, if he got me some toys. You know, something to make it a bit more exciting."

"I take it we're not talking train sets or Matthew's junior Meccano here, then Caroline?" said Beryl laughing.

"No, no," she hushed her voice. "I mean sex toys. You know the kind of thing you see at Ann Summers parties." She leaned in close to the table. "He bought me a vibrator."

"A vibrator!" squealed her mum at the top of her voice. "Good for him."

"Shush Mum, keep your voice down I don't want the whole village knowing!"

"Well, I'm sorry love, but I just think that's hilarious."

"It's called a Rabbit," she continued. "And I swear to God when I took it out the box, I nearly screamed. It looked like something out of Doctor Who!"

"I've heard about them, they're supposed to be good. Have you taken it on a test run yet?" Beryl said with a glint in her eye.

"No, I bloody haven't! I haven't been able to face it yet, scary looking bugger. And as for the instructions, well, I felt like I was back taking GCSE biology again. I didn't know whether I was meant to use it with Andrew or if he was hoping I would get in some practice on my own and give him a shout when I was up for it!"

"I don't think it matters love," said her mum. "I used to use mine for both with yer dad."

Everyone except Caroline burst out laughing.

"Oh, now, thanks a bunch Mum. There's an image your child should never have to think of, too much information, too much information!"

"I don't see why," chirped Babs. "It's no worse than me having to listen to you telling stories about your sex life is it?"

"She's got a point," said Beryl. "Works both ways, you know."

"Apparently so," giggled Jean

"I didn't mean it like that, God you've got a one track mind you have Jean," laughed Beryl.

"I couldn't be bothered," said Jean. "I mean, don't get me wrong, I still enjoy my delving under the duvet, but introducing battery operated gadgets into the bedroom... Well, it would scare the shit out the dog." (He slept on the bed, apparently.)

I was totally taken aback by the conversation we were having, amazed that Caroline was willing to discuss her sexual problems in front of her mum. I could never have done that with mine.

"What about you Jo, do you indulge in naughty toys?" asked Jean.

"No," I said. "No, we don't do anything like that."

"Well, I think as long as you're both happy doing what you like to do, it doesn't matter," said Beryl.

"Yeah, well, we all know what you and Bill like to do, now don't we?" chirped Jean.

"Shush Jean, don't you be telling all my secrets, you cheeky cow."

"So what's George into then?" pushed Jean. "I bet being away as much as he is you're at it like rabbits when he gets back, eh eh." She nudged me in the arm.

I didn't know what to say. I would never dream of discussing my sex life with anyone but, I was a little worse for wear and the wine had made me loose lipped. I took a deep breath.

"Actually, we don't do sex any more, In fact, not only do we not do sex, but we haven't done sex for over five years." My speech was slightly slurred. "That's got you all thinking now hasn't it?" I raised my glass and took a large gulp of wine. "Cheers!"

The table went very quiet.

"Bloody hell Jo, that's quite a statement, don't you like sex?" Beryl's voice was concerned.

"Nope," I said. "I don't think I do."

"Five years!" said Jean incredulously. "Christ, I would have gone mad by now. Either that or me and the dog would have become really good friends. I couldn't go that long!"

"Oh, I don't know," said Caroline. "I can see how it could happen. Although I'd hate to think I'd gone off it forever. Five years?" she said, looking worried. "Perhaps I'll give this vibrator thing a go after all."

Even in my drunken state I could tell they were all shocked.

"Well, some women just don't have much of a libido do they?" Beryl was trying to be reassuring. "Not all women are randy old slappers like us. Who's to say what's normal and what's not eh?" She put her arm around my shoulder and gave me a hug.

"I don't mean to sound unsympathetic," said Jean. "But I'm pretty sure five years isn't normal, not unless you've made a conscious decision to become celibate. It that what it is Jo, you decided to be celibate?"

"Jean!" chastised Beryl.

"I'm sorry," she said defensively. "I'm not trying to make you feel, bad or wrong or anything Jo, I'm sure you and George show you love each other in lots of different ways. Nice hugs and kisses and things I bet?"

"Nope," I said. "We never hug or kiss."

"But don't you get urges?" She continued. She was apparently finding the whole thing quite mind boggling. "The idea of no physical contact, I don't know how you can stand it."

"Jean, pack it in, you're making Jo feel like some kind of freak, now stop it." Beryl was serious in her firmness.

"No, no, it's fine," I said. "She's right, I'm sure it's not normal, I don't have any urges. I just don't ever think about it."

Caroline was looking very concerned for me. "But Jo," she said earnestly, "if you don't ever make love, or have hugs and kisses, that means you must never feel loved."

Out of all the things said, bless her youth; that was possibly the comment that hit home the most. She was right, I didn't ever feel loved. I took another glug of wine.

"That's not all," I slurred. "I found out yesterday that my dick of a husband is shagging someone else. Ha, top that if you can." I raised my glass in the air again. "Cheers girls, welcome to the world of Marjorie Primm."

There was a shocked unison of, "What", "No" and "Oh, Jo".

I then told them about finding the receipts and how I had decided not to confront George about it.

"The lying, cheating bastard," said Jean. "I'd dress him up in his fancy underwear and string him up by the balls if he were mine."

"No," I said. "I can't blame him; he's bound to go looking elsewhere if I'm not interested. It's not his fault."

"He could have tried talking to you about it," said Caroline.

She had a point. He could have.

"It's not that easy for us," I said. "We're not like you guys, we don't have that openness to our relationship, and neither of us can talk about these things."

"Well, you're talking to us now," said Beryl.

"Yeah, but that's because I'm pissed," I said.

"Well, perhaps that's what you need to do with George," said Babs. "Get rat arsed one night and jump on him when he least expects it. I always like doing that to Frank when the golf's on. I consider it a real test of my womanly charms if I can manage to seduce him whilst the golf's on. It's one of the little challenges I set myself to keep me on my toes." Her comments made us all chuckle and brought lightness back to the group that was much needed.

"Muuum," said Caroline. "Too much information, Agaaaa-in."

"I don't think it matters anymore," I said. "I just want to make sure Rebecca isn't affected by it."

"Well, I think you're very brave," said Caroline. "I would fall apart if my Andrew ever did anything like that to me."

"Ah well," I said. "That's because you love him."

"And don't you love George?" said Beryl.

Up to that point I hadn't consciously thought about it. But when I did, when I seriously looked inside myself and tried to think about how I felt, there just wasn't any feeling there.

"No," I said. "I really don't think I do."

"God, this is so depressing," said Jean. "Jo, if you're ada-mant that you're not going to ditch this emotional loser, we need to make sure you start having some fun. Agreed girls?" She raised her glass in the air.

A resounding "Agreed!" went up, followed by a loud clash of glasses and a good amount of spilt wine.

"But you hardly know me," I said. "Why on earth should you care whether I am happy or not?"

"Listen hun," said Beryl. "Anyone who sticks Helena's class for more than two weeks running has to be a little bit special. You're one of us now, so tough." Again she gave me the reassuring arm round the shoulder hug. This was an extraor-dinary group of woman and I felt honoured that they now counted me as one of them.

Babs gave an unexpected squeak and shouted. "Oh, oh, I've missed something important here Jo."

"What's that?" I said.

"Too many Bacardis I'm afraid, I think I'm still catching up on conversations from about ten minutes ago. Sorry, blonde moment going on. You said the receipts from George's hotel were in Leeds right?"

"Yes, why?"

"Which one, which one?" She was getting quite excited.

"It was Malmaison," I said.

"Shit, I don't believe it," she cried. "My best friend is one of the housekeepers there, I could probably find out who the lying snake was with if you like. I can put her on the alert to tell us if it happens again."

My God, I wondered, do I really want to know? What if it was someone we knew, what if it was someone in the village? Or worse still someone sat at this table!

"I, I'm not sure," I stammered. My thinking didn't take long. "Yes, yes, find out anything you can, the dates were 14th to 17th June."

"Bloody brilliant," said Babs. "I feel like James fucking Bond."

I wasn't sure whether it was the right thing to do, but what the hell, what was the worst that could happen?

The evening rolled on with us getting steadily drunk and increasingly sillier. For some reason I will never understand, I decided to get up and do a rendition of "*I am what I am*" when they started karaoke, it was not a pretty sight. If the village had forgotten who I was the night before, they were certainly going to remember who I was by the morning after.

The evening reached a natural conclusion when our inability to string complete sentences together became too much of a hindrance to ordering drinks. Beryl made the call to Bill and we stood outside waiting for him to collect us. Hugs were exchanged with the other girls and we all parted company. I felt a slight twinge of fear, would this somehow come back to haunt me. That these people were not my friends at all and I had been completely wrong to trust them.

Bill arrived in the Land Rover.

"Oh dear, oh dear," he said. "Looks like you've had a good night then, girls."

"We have my love," said Beryl. "We most certainly have."

We clambered into the Land Rover and went the few short miles to the farmhouse. Once we got in, we both slumped into a rather nice plump sofa that was at the far end of the kitchen facing an open fire gently glowing in the grate.

"Well, it looks like I have some catching up to do," said Bill. "Anyone for more rhubarb wine?"

"No thanks," I said. "But I could murder a coffee."

"No, not for me Bill," said Beryl. "I'll join Jo in a coffee."

"Two coffees, coming up," he grinned.

"My Bill is fab," said Beryl. "You could do a lot worse than getting yourself a man like my Bill. He's so kind and considerate, and he loves me so much. He'd do anything for me would my Bill."

"He is very lovely," I said. "I don't suppose he has a brother?"

"'Fraid not," she sighed. "He has got a sister in Plymouth, but I guess that's not quite the same. Besides, I bet her husband wouldn't be too keen."

We both burst out laughing.

Bill came over to see what was so funny. "Now then girls. What you two up to?"

"Oh, not much," said Beryl. "I was just telling Jo that she could do with a man like you, she's having a few problems with her fella, and he's been neglecting his husbandly duties, well with Jo anyway. He's been dipping his wick elsewhere."

"Beryl!" I said, dismayed. "Don't tell Bill my troubles. I'm sure he's not remotely interested."

"Oh Jo," he said with real concern. "I'm very sorry to hear that."

"Nah, don't worry about it." I waved my arm. "It's OK, I don't care anymore. I think that side of me has taken early retirement. The motherly, housekeeping bits still fully employed though, so it really doesn't matter."

"Well, he's a very stupid man then. I'll go and get the coffees." He wandered off to another part of the kitchen.

"See," I told you. "My Bill is such a sweetie." She spoke in a drowsy dreamy kind of voice.

"You're very, very, very, lucky," I slurred.

Bill came back with the coffees and his bottle of rhubarb wine; we chatted about the night's events and after a while a rather nice home-made plum brandy was produced. With hindsight, this was possibly not the best plan as despite my protests Beryl insisted on filling Bill in on the state of my sex life.

"To my mind," said Beryl, "the only reason a woman would go off sex is if it was crap. It's not just a one way street you know Jo, he has to give as good as he gets. I mean, why else would you not want to do it?"

"I don't know," I said. "I've never thought about it."

"Well, think about it now. Was George an attentive and giving lover?"

"I suppose he was," I paused. "He used to pull my nightie down when he'd finished, I always thought that was very considerate."

"You are joking, right?" said Beryl.

"Yes Beryl," I sighed. "That was a joke."

"Thank God for that, you had me worried there for a minute. So he was OK then, always used to make sure you were satisfied as well as him? You know, that you came too?"

"Ah well," I said. "He might of thought I did, I always used to fake that bit."

Bill was sitting listening to the conversation, in quiet contemplation.

"But he didn't know you well enough to know whether you had or you hadn't then?" Bill asked.

"I suppose not."

"Typical bloody man," said Beryl. "Present company excepted, my love."

"That's OK hun, I know what you mean."

"So have you never, ever come then Jo, either when you've had sex or by other means?"

"I don't think I have."

"Bloody hell!" she exclaimed. "That husband of yours wants taking out and shooting."

I laughed. "I don't see what you're getting so upset about Beryl; it's not like I'm bothered. I've told you I just don't get that kind of urge."

"Sounds to me as though you just haven't had the right buttons pressed," said Bill

"Oh, and he'd know," said Beryl. "He's a very good button presser is our Bill. Bet you could re-start Jo's engine for her, couldn't you my love?"

"Oh, I don't know about that, love."

"See, beautiful man and modest with it. How lucky am I?" She got up and went and gave him a passionate open mouthed kiss. I looked away, embarrassed.

"I think it's time I went to bed," I said. "Leave you two love birds alone."

"Nonsense, let's have another brandy." She staggered to the table and retrieved the bottle and topped up our glasses.

"So what are you going to do Jo?" asked Bill.

"I honestly don't know, it's all a bit confusing."

"What you need, my girl, is a good sorting out, that would set your head straight and I know just the man to do it."

"Beryl..." Bill's voice was slow and cautious.

She stood up violently, sloshing her brandy on the floor as she swung her arms about.

"No, I'm serious. I am the proud owner of a man who gives the best orgasms in the county and this woman has never had an orgasm in her life. Now where would my sense of sisterhood be if I didn't think that was something I should share, eh, well, eh?"

"Beryl," I said calmly. "I think you'd better sit down. It's a very, very kind offer, but you really wouldn't want me to have sex with your husband, now would you?"

"Who said anything about sex; all I'm suggesting is that he shows you how it should be done and you don't need to have sex to do that. There's more than one way to skin a cat, so to speak. Shows how much you don't know girl. At least if you let Bill have a go you'd have a pretty good idea of what to look for next time, you'll have a bench mark to go by."

"Do I get a say in this?" said Bill

"No my love, you don't. Consider it to be an act of charity."

"Great," I said. "Is that how you see me, a charity case? Charming!"

"No, no, you're missing the point." She sat back down. "Look, think of it like this. What if I had a nice dress or jumper that you liked. Something that if you wore it, would make you feel really good about yourself. Would you borrow it?"

"I'm pretty sure you can't liken Bill to a jumper Beryl. That's just wrong."

"No, it isn't," she retorted. "I'm saying you can borrow him, not that you can keep him. A once in a lifetime, one night only offer. He's bloody good at what he does and I'm telling you girl if he can't get you started again, then your engine's seized up."

"Beryl, you're not making any sense, you've had too much to drink and you're not thinking straight. Bill I am so sorry, this must be so embarrassing for you."

"Not really, I'm rather flattered if the truth be told, what man wouldn't be."

My God, what have I got myself into here? Either the woman has no morals or she's a bloody genius.

"Well, I am off to bed," she said. "You two can stay down here and have a little chat. Bill, if you or she gets the urge, go for it, but I don't want to know anything about it, and you don't go as far as having sex. OK?"

She got up, went over to him, gave him a big kiss and disappeared upstairs. There was an awkward silence; neither of us quite knew what to say.

Bill was the first one to speak. "Can I get you anything else, More coffee?"

"That's probably a good idea," I said. "Thank you."

He went and got us both a cup and came and sat beside me on the sofa.

"Don't let Beryl upset you Jo, she does mean well."

"I'm sure she does," I said. "But you have to admit it's not normal is it, to offer the use of your husband to a woman you hardly know?"

"Ah well, our Beryl is no ordinary woman."

The conversation paused and we drank our coffee.

"So is that all true Jo, the stuff about George, I mean?"

"I'm afraid so."

"And are you honestly going to stay with him then, even after finding out what he's done?"

"What else can I do?" I said.

"Find someone else," he said. "You're a good looking woman you know, I'm sure you'd be snapped up in no time."

"That's very sweet of you, but I'm pretty sure that's not true. Anyway, I don't think I could be bothered, far too much hassle."

He leaned over and very softly swept a section of my hair to one side. "You clearly don't think very highly of yourself, do you?"

"I, I don't suppose I do," I said nervously.

"Well, I think we need to work on that." Before I even had chance to register what was happening, he reached over and kissed me, a soft gentle kiss on the lips.

"I don't' think you should do that, do you?" I said, moving to the other side of the sofa.

"Oh trust me, you don't need to worry about Beryl. She meant every word she said, she's a very giving person is our Beryl."

He took my hand.

"I'd like to kiss you again, that is unless you don't want me to."

"I, I don't know," I said. My head was spinning; the whole situation was just bizarre. I knew I should say no. That I should get up and leave, go to bed and sneak out in the morning and hope I never saw either of them again. But the wine, the brandy and Beryl's frankness about sex had set my mind racing. The new me, the adventurous me was becoming stronger and stronger. The alcohol had weakened my sense of right and wrong and I was lost in the moment. Bill's voice was so soft and warm and his touch so gentle. I found myself feeling as though I was melting from the inside. Could he rekindle in me something I had lost? I was starting to feel as though he could.

"Would you mind just kissing me again?" I said quietly.

"Certainly." He reached over and gave me another gentle kiss, this time it was more sensual, I could feel his tongue gently trying to probe into my mouth. It felt delicious.

64

"Should I stop?" he said.

"No, not just yet," I said breathlessly. "Perhaps just once more to know for sure."

He leant over again. This time I allowed him to probe my mouth with his tongue. Deep, gentle thrusts that made my head whirl. No one had ever kissed me like that.

"Verdict?" he said.

"Jury's out."

"Better try harder, then." He smiled.

He got up and went and knelt on the rug in front of the fire, holding out his hand he gently guided me to the floor. I lay down and allowed him to seduce me. He began by kissing my neck and shoulders, tender kisses and delicate nibbles, it was sublime. His touch was so sensual, so gentle, soft caressing fingertips, coupled with passionate sexual kisses. I had feelings inside me that I had never felt before, or if I had it had been so long ago that I'd forgotten.

"Can I go further?" he asked.

I was gone completely gone; this man was unbelievable and I was ready to take whatever he could give me.

"Yes, yes," I gasped. "Do whatever you want!"

He slowly unbuttoned my shirt, and with one hand deftly undid my bra, an act in itself to be admired. I wriggled free of the clothing and lay on the floor half naked, wondering what else he would do to me. He took his shirt off, revealing a surprisingly well toned torso and lay beside me.

The next hour was spent in hitherto inexperienced bliss. Bill did things to me that I didn't even realise could be done. His fingers found parts of me that I didn't even know I had and when I finally came it was such a revelation, I cried.

I didn't know what else to do. All those years of pent up emotion just poured out of me and I sat and cried.

Bill wasn't fazed by this at all, he simply held me and softly kissed my hair until I'd calmed down.

"I'm lost for words," I said. "Thank you somehow sounds wrong, but thank you - that was amazing."

"You don't need to thank me," he whispered. "I'm just glad I made you happy for a while."

Happy? Happy, you nearly blew my head off!

He cradled me in his arms and we sat and talked by the dying embers of the fire for a while. I was amazed by how calm he was about the whole thing. There was no awkwardness and no rushing to leave me, just a real feeling of concern and compassion.

I concluded that Beryl and Bill were a most unusual couple. But what the hell would happen in the morning?

7

Unexpected Repercussions

When Bill and I had finally gone up to bed, I fell asleep pretty quickly. I drifted off contentedly in the little single bed, warmly remembering the sensations I had just experienced.

I had no feelings of guilt or remorse, just a lovely butterfly feeling in my stomach indicative of doing something that made you excited.

When I woke up in the morning, those wonderful feelings had gone. I had a vague moment of peace, then my brain kicked in and whacked me with a sledgehammer of realisation.

Shit, I thought. Shit, shit, shit. How stupid can one person really be?

I cringed with embarrassment as I remembered the conversations of the previous evening and the actions that subsequently followed.

For crying out loud woman, what were you thinking? You have one night out and your whole sense of morality goes out the bloody window. Why, oh why, did I let it happen? Bloody drink, I knew there was a reason I kept well away from it. Clearly, it made me behave like a complete and utter slapper.

I got dressed and sat on the edge of the bed. I still had butterflies in my stomach, but now they were caused by sheer terror. Oh my God, how on earth am I going to face Beryl and Bill? There was no way I could avoid it, I couldn't just run out the door, as much as I might have wanted to. I was just going to have to brave it out so I went downstairs.

Beryl was in the kitchen frying bacon. There was no sign of Bill.

"Morning Beryl," I said sheepishly.

"Good morning love," she beamed. "Did you sleep well?"

"Yes, Yes, I did, thank you." I sat at the table.

I was watching her closely, looking for any sign that showed she might be annoyed or upset. I could detect nothing.

"Well, I don't know about you," she said. "But I needs a big fat fry up before I does anything else today. So how do you like your eggs?"

"Oh no, not for me, thanks, I don't think I could face it." All I wanted was to get out of there as fast as I could.

"You sure? Aw dodgy stomach 'ave you? That's not surprising after what you knocked back last night. I'm sorry love I should have kept a closer eye on you; I knew you hadn't had a drink for a while."

"No, it's fine," I said. "It's entirely my own fault, I should know better."

"Well, not to worry, as long as you had a good night, I know I did. Think we might have overdone it with the brandy though, I can't remember a bloody thing that happened once we got home. You wants a coffee Jo?"

Bugger, I panicked, she doesn't remember. How can she not remember, she must do. How can you spend an hour trying to persuade your husband to sexually pleasure another woman and then just let it just slip your mind? It was unbelievable! What kind of person would forget something as off the wall as that? And aside from that how could she be so inconsiderate? I had spent ages psyching myself up for dealing with the aftermath; I had all sorts of different speeches rehearsed in my head dependant on how she had reacted.

There was the, "I'm incredibly sorry. I will leave the village immediately never to return and I promise I will never see you or Bill again," speech.

The "Yes, he was bloody fantastic; thank you so much for loaning him to me for the night; I'm going straight off to find one just like him," speech.

I had even contemplated the likelihood of my being able to duck fast enough had the frying pan been hurled at my head upon entering the room; but no, it seemed she had forgotten the whole thing.

Oh no, this was terrible. This wasn't what I thought would happen at all.

So what was I supposed to do now? Think, think, I told myself. I'll come clean, surely the best thing is to be upfront and honest about it and apologise?

I thought again.

And tell her what, you stupid cow! That you took her at her word and truly believed her drunken proposal was serious? That you had it away with her husband, hoping she would remember and be all hunky-dory about it. Not very likely.

Well...I pondered.

If she unbelievably has forgotten, perhaps the best thing I could do is say nothing. Yes, that's it, keep schtum and don't mention it unless she does. Act normal, pretend everything's fine and hope to God Bill doesn't walk through that door. Oh no, Bill, what about poor Bill? Hang on a minute, why poor Bill? I didn't kiss him, he kissed me. Perhaps he was also so drunk he wouldn't remember.

My mind was racing.

No hang on, he hadn't been drinking all night. He didn't start until we came back in, he was quite sober, he must remember. What kind of man was he then? Would he realise she had forgotten her offer and as a good honest husband feel obliged to tell her? Oh God, maybe he already had and she was just testing me to see what I would do.

Where was he anyway?

Was he so mortified by what had happened that he couldn't face me? Or was it Beryl? Had she perhaps flown off the handle and done something to him. Was he in the barn somewhere chopped into little pieces? Oh no, is she just biding her time and then she's going to get me too!

I was starting to panic; my little brain just wasn't used to dealing with this level of complexity. I was Marjorie Primm, for Christ's sake. The most complex thing I usually had to deal with was what to cook for tea! How on earth was I expected to unravel this immoral maze, especially at this time on a Saturday morning.

Oh swallow me up, please ground swallow me up. I don't want to be here anymore. What a mess, what a complete and utter sodding mess. I felt sick, I just wanted to get out that house and run home.

"Jo?" It was Beryl's voice. I was so startled out of my own thoughts that I gave a little scream.

"By, you were miles away there girl, you all right? You look ever so pale." She seemed genuinely concerned.

"Yes, yes, I'm fine," I said. "I, I think I should get going Beryl, George will play hell if I don't get back."

"Oh, that's a shame love. Sure you don't want a quick coffee?"

"No, honestly, I'm fine. Thank you." I got up, grabbed my bag and went for the door.

"Err, hang on a minute Mrs," she said firmly.

My heart leapt into my mouth. Hell, this is it. I turned round half expecting to see her brandishing a carving knife, but she wasn't, she was holding out her arms.

"Don't I get a hug?" She walked over and gave me a big squeeze.

"Oh Beryl, I'm sorry," I said. "I don't know what's wrong with me this morning. My head seems to be all over the place."

"Well, you get yourself home lass and take it easy, let that husband of yours fend for himself for a day." She opened the door.

"Bye then," I said.

"Bye, bye love, see you Thursday if not before."

I waved as I went across the yard and got into the car.

You're a bitch, I said to myself, a complete and utter bitch. You say you're desperate for friends and what's the first thing you do when you get one? Shag her bloody husband that's what. It's no wonder George never lets you out. You're a threat to common decency! I was totally ashamed of myself. If this was who the new me was turning out to be, I needed to seriously reconsider my plan. I drove off thinking I had never felt so relieved to get away from a place in my life.

I pulled into our drive feeling dreadful. I was a terrible liar and felt sure that if George even asked the vaguest of questions about my evening he would somehow know that I had been up to no good. Thankfully, his car wasn't there.

I went into the house, to find a note pinned on the wall in the hall. It read

Taken Rebecca to get some lunch, we couldn't wait for you any longer. G.

Arse, was opening the fridge genuinely such a challenge?

I made a coffee and went and had a cigarette behind the greenhouse. I took long draws in hoping it would make me calmer. It kind of worked.

I ran a bath, and clambered into the warm bubbly water. Despite my hatred of myself for what I had done, I couldn't get Bill and his amazing touch out of my head. I kept going over and over the way he had pleasured me the previous evening, reliving the sensations. It made me feel light headed and incredibly aroused.

I got out of the bath, dried myself; and then laid on the bed. With the thoughts of Bill still very much in my mind, I constructed a beautiful, sensual, erotic fantasy about the man that had rekindled my desire and did something I had never, ever done in my life before, I masturbated. One luscious orgasm later, I dreamily fell asleep.

I woke up an hour later to find George and Rebecca were still not home. I got dressed and went downstairs prepared to get on with my chores of the day.

A quick check of my emails and Facebook first, I decided.

I logged on. There was one email from Helena with the list for next week's class. On Facebook there were some rather dreadful photos of us out as a group that Caroline had posted from her phone. Oh God, I thought, I look like a real lush! I posted a suitably disapproving comment back to her and checked through postings from other people.

I went to the panto page first, they used it to post details of rehearsals and meetings. There were a couple of notices about rehearsal times and then some photos which Imelda Falthrop had posted from one of her theatre trips to Leeds.

I couldn't put my finger on why, but I just could not bring myself to like this woman. Effusively loud at all times, she seemed to believe that the whole world wanted to hear everything she had to say. I wondered how her husband could possibly put up with her, he seemed such a nice quiet chap and the complete opposite of her. I assumed it likely we both had the same problem; domineering and overpowering spouses.

Considering my own indiscretions, I made an attempt to be of generous spirit and decided my real reason for disliking her so much was because I was jealous. She was so confident, positively oozed self-belief and possessed all the qualities I could never hope to have.

Mainly for bitching purposes I continued, glancing through her photos. One that particularly caught my eye was of her stood outside her hotel. She was immaculately dressed in what was clearly some little designer number, obviously on her way out for the evening. She had her arm in the air in a 'Statue of Liberty' kind of stance and was looking very pleased with herself.

"You posey cow," I said.

Then I noticed the name of the hotel. It was Malmaison.

Oh great, like I needed reminding of that. Blah, tacky horrid people, wonder if she's ever seen George there?

It set me thinking about his infidelity again. I did sort of feel I had balanced the books a bit, but was not at all happy with how I had gone about it. I was no better than him now.

I decided that sooner rather than later I needed to speak to Bill. I wanted to get his take on things and ask his advice on what I should do about Beryl. I was prepared to do whatever needed to be done to try and set this straight. This woman had been unbelievably kind to me and I was not going to do anything further that could hurt her. Despite having incredibly powerful feelings for Bill, he was not mine and nor could he ever be. He had done me a great service and I was sure that the puppy dog feelings I had were no more than the equivalent of a schoolgirl crush. I might have rediscovered my sexual yearnings, but I was just going to have to find another way to deal with them.

I went on Google and typed in 'Rampant Rabbits'. A few clicks later and I had one ordered. That should keep my lustful yearnings at bay, for now at least.

I wonder, does using someone else's husband as a masturbation fantasy constitute being unfaithful? There was an interesting philosophical debate for the next girls' night out; assuming that I would still be invited and that they wouldn't have tarred and feathered me by then.

I signed off the computer and had just gone back into the kitchen when I heard the front door open. It was George and Rebecca.

Rebecca came bouncing into the kitchen. "Hello Mummy, did you have a lovely evening? Daddy took me to McDonald's for lunch. He was ever so funny he couldn't get the hang of how it all worked. Don't think fast food is his thing do you?"

"No darling, I don't think it is."

George came in looking very annoyed. "Bloody stupid place," he said. "What kind of way is that to run a business?"

I smiled, "A very successful one, I'd say George."

"Oh, don't start being clever with me Marjorie, I'm not in the mood. Where the hell were you this morning anyway? You said you were away for the night not the whole bloody weekend!"

"Sorry dear, it ended up being a bit of a session so I was up late this morning. Did you two have a good night last night?"

"We did Mummy, we had popcorn and everything. It was really good fun."

"That's good, I'm glad. See George, no harm done. The world is still turning; civilisation as we know it has not ceased to be just because I went out for an evening."

"That's not the point, Marjorie and you know it!"

Bless him, I do believe he is quite cross.

"Mummy, is it all right if I go up to my room? Dad bought me some new CD's whilst we were out and I want to play them."

"Course it is hun, I'll give you a shout when dinner's ready."

Rebecca disappeared and George and I were left alone in the kitchen.

"Well, all I can say Marjorie, is that I don't want you making a habit of this going out business. Your place is here, not living it up at the local pubs."

He sounded very firm. His reaction, I thought, was a little OTT even for George. I couldn't help wondering if there was another reason he didn't want me going out.

Got it! I said to myself. He doesn't want me going out in case I see him and his fancy piece together. He's annoyed because I might start cramping his style. He's so used to gadding about without having to cover his tracks and he's worried now that he might have to start being careful, the sly old dog.

"Well, all I can say," I retorted. "Is that I will be doing it at least once a month George, whether you like it or not!"

"Marjorie, I am telling you, I am not going to stand for this kind of inappropriate behaviour!"

"Oh calm down George, your veins are starting to pop. What do you suppose you can do to stop me, chain me up in the cellar?" I paused. "Actually, thinking about it, I might quite like that."

"Marjorie! That's quite enough of that. I don't know what's come over you lately, but I don't like it," he rebuked.

I was quite enjoying this exchange, it was lovely to see George getting so irate and for once being able to understand the real reason behind it. I couldn't resist taking things a step further.

I went up to him softly, placing my hands on his chest. The look of shock that I'd dared to touch him was priceless.

"Oh, George," I said. "I'm sorry, it's just it's been so long since you and I did anything together and I get so lonely out here. Couldn't we have a weekend away somewhere? I'm sure that would do wonders for settling me back down. I know I've been a little out of sorts lately, I don't mean to be."

"Yes, well, that's as maybe." He removed my hands from his chest. "But it's still no way to behave. I will have a think about the weekend away; perhaps we could go and see my mother in Sussex."

"Oh no George," I said. "I was thinking more of a luxury hotel somewhere, you know just you and me, like we used to. Romantic dinner for two, we could even go see a show. Leeds has some great things coming up over the next few weeks, a friend of mine was telling me. She's just come back from there, had a fabulous time by all accounts and stayed in a lovely hotel, she did tell me the name of it, now God what was it?" I pretended to struggle for the name.

"Err, err, it's on the tip of my tongue, something French sounding I think, God my French never was any good. What's the name for house in French, George? Oh, hang on I've got it: Malmaison," I said. "That was it. Malmaison."

The colour visibly drained from his face and I had to bite my lip to stop myself laughing.

"Supposed to be very swish," I continued. "Do you know it George? Have you ever been there?"

"Why on earth would I have been there?" he said defensively.

"Oh I don't know, you go to so many different hotels with work. I just thought that might have been one of them."

"No, No," he said swiftly. "Never been there, definitely not."

"I'll get a brochure then, shall I? We can see what it's like. Just let me know what dates you're free, I'm sure Rebecca can stay at a friend's house for a night."

"Right, yes, fine," he said. "Now if you'll excuse me, I have some work to do, Oh and don't bother with dinner for me, I'm not hungry." He shot out of the room.

No I bet you're not, I thought.

I heard him pour a whisky from the decanter on the side in the dining room, before the study door slammed shut. I knew exactly what he would be doing; he would be sitting trying to work out if my comments were innocent or if I had twigged he'd been cheating. Poor George, it's a good job he doesn't have a weak heart.

I went to bed that night and reflected on the bizarre events of the last few days. So much had happened.

My trip to the library had seemed to act as some sort of catalyst to my life being turned upside down. I may have wanted to make some changes to my day to day routine, but I am not sure adultery and secret sexual encounters were quite what I had in mind. Still, 'in for a penny, in for a pound'. I can't reverse it and pretend it hasn't happened. Tomorrow I will go to panto rehearsal and on Monday I will try and get hold of Bill. Damage limitation required there, I think.

George was going away again on Sunday evening for a week and I couldn't help wondering if he was genuinely due in Brussels on Sunday night or whether he was having a little stop-over in Leeds first. One thing was for sure though; I bet he'd been searching high and low for the last hotel bill. Not knowing what I knew would be driving him mad.

When I got up on Sunday morning, I was surprised to find that he had already packed; his cases were by the front door and he was sitting in the living room, going through some papers.

"Morning George," I said. "I thought you weren't leaving until tonight."

"Yes, well, change of plan, a client needs to see me urgently before I leave, so I said I could squeeze them in before I fly out."

He seemed less confident than usual, a little flustered. He's lying, I decided.

"That's a shame, Rebecca will be sorry you're leaving early, have you said goodbye to her?"

"No, she's still asleep and I didn't want to wake her. Tell her I said goodbye though, and give her a big hug and a kiss from me."

Strange, he's not usually that bothered.

"Have you had breakfast?"

"No, No, Don't worry about it." He was hastily stuffing papers into his briefcase. "I'll get something later. I need to get going."

"And you're back a week today, is that right?"

"Yes, yes, all being well."

"OK, then," I said resolutely. "Well, have a safe trip and I'll speak to you later in the week."

He went to the front door and collected his cases. I went into the kitchen and watched out of the window as he loaded them into the car.

Hang on a minute; that seems to be an awful lot of luggage for a week away. Normally he just takes a large holdall and his suit carrier. Why has he got two suitcases? I pondered on it as I watched. George was oblivious to the fact I was even there. He seemed distracted.

Oh my God, I bet he's leaving me! I panicked and felt slightly nauseous. He wouldn't surely; he wouldn't just walk out without telling me? I nearly rushed out to the car to ask him, but rationality told me to stop being so stupid. So I let him go. I waved and smiled out of the window as he drove off.

He didn't even look back.

Rebecca and I had a quiet morning, both of us possibly a little anxious about the forthcoming event of the afternoon. With everything that had gone on, I was beginning to think that pushing myself to tread the boards was not one of my brightest ideas. I had no talent, I couldn't sing, Friday night had proved that and my dancing skills were totally non-existent. No, I decided that rather than making a complete and utter fool of myself, I would offer my services backstage instead.

We arrived at the Town Hall and Rebecca went and found her friends. I found a suitably inconspicuous spot on a chair at the side of the hall and contemplated the doom of my fate. To compound my fear further several people came up to chat to me, which although was extremely kind, confirmed my suspicion that mature members of the chorus were somewhat of a rarity.

Most of the adults involved were hard core thesps who spent their free time flitting from one production to another as and when required. Great: so there's me, a game old bird in her 70s called Sheila, and 20 children aged between 8 and 16.

Sheila apparently had been involved since it started 20 odd years ago, but never wanted a main part, she enjoyed being on the back row.

"I do it for the social side of it, dear," she told me.

Nope, be sensible, the odds are stacked against me, I am definitely going to volunteer for backstage.

Ian Henderson arrived and came and said hello to me. Then the business of the afternoon began.

"Imelda sends her apologies, but she has unfortunately been delayed," announced Ian. "But, she will be here before the end of rehearsal. We can still make a start though. If you would all like to pull up a chair and form a circle, we'll have a read through of the script so you can get a feel for your parts."

We all did as we were asked and the read through began, It was surprisingly good fun. People were laughing at the script and at each other if they fluffed their lines or tried a funny voice, but it was all in good spirit. True, there was a fair smattering of the luvvie brigade, but there were also some genuinely talented people.

When we had read as far as the interval in the script we stopped: tea, coffee and biscuits were magically produced for everyone. It was whilst we were drinking our coffee that Imelda burst through the double doors of the hall. Swathed in a bright red pashmina, she stood with her arms in her usual wide open gesture.

"Darlings, darlings, I am soooo sorry I am late, so terribly remiss of me and at the first rehearsal too."

She flounced over to Ian, threw her arms around him and gave him a kiss on both cheeks. "So kind of you to get things started for me Ian, but it's OK now everyone, I am here."

She did a round of the principles, lots of hugs, lots of kisses and lots of very loud talking.

"Right, let's get on and read through Act II, shall we? See just how much work I've got cut out for me, eh?"

Everybody went back to their places. I decided it would be better to tell her that I was not up for my debut, before we went any further.

I stood at the side of her chair. "Imelda," I said softly. "Could I have a word?"

"Oh, hello," she said rather dismissively. "Marjorie isn't it?"

"Yes, yes, it is – well Jo, actually."

"Right, yes, well what can I do for you?"

"Well, you see, I've been thinking and I'm not sure I'm cut out to be on stage. I was wondering if I could help backstage instead, if that would be OK?"

I couldn't believe how nervous this woman made me feel. I was totally intimidated by her.

"No, dear," she bellowed. "I'm afraid that's just not possible, already cast the chorus you see, choreographed the numbers and everything. I'd have to change everyone round if you dropped out now and I'm sorry, but I'm just not prepared to do that."

"Oh," I said. "I see. I'm sorry, I hadn't realised."

"No, well, you newbies, you just don't realise what's involved do you?" Her tone was extraordinarily patronising.

"No, apparently not," I said. "Right then." I went and sat back down.

Bugger, that didn't go quite the way I expected. Bit harsh I thought. Perhaps I could just drop out altogether, after all, what's the worst she could do? Hunt me down and kill me for crimes against panto! I glanced across at her and concluded that yes, actually, she probably would.

We read through Act II, but somehow it didn't seem as funny as Act I.

"Right then, well that was fairly mediocre, I'd say," said Imelda. "Principles, please read your scripts over and over. Get to know your characters. You need to eat, sleep and breathe the person you are."

God, this woman is unbelievably obnoxious. Why on earth do people put up with her? Then I remembered my own flustering at confronting her. Fear, I concluded, pure unadulterated cowardice.

"We will start blocking Act 1, Scene 1, on Thursday," she continued. "If you're not in that scene you don't need to be here. Chorus, we need you for an hour between 6.30pm and 7.30pm. Thank you; that will be all."

We left the hall and Rebecca and I drove home. She was fine, excited and greatly looking forward to the next rehearsal. I was thinking how the hell I could get out of this without incurring the wrath of Imelda Falthrop and knew that I possibly couldn't.

8

Swings and Roundabouts

Monday dawned and I considered what I needed to do that week. I knew I had to get in touch with Bill but in a way that would not make Beryl suspicious. God, I wished I was better at this manipulation and deceit stuff. I wondered if they did online courses in it these days. Bet they do. Note to self...check out courses on how to be a complete bitch.

I eventually came up with the pretext of ringing her to check what we were doing on Thursday. I was physically shaking when I dialled and my heart was racing.

"Fell View Farm." It was Beryl's warm, gentle voice.

"Hi Beryl, it's Jo." I was trying so hard to sound light and casual. "How are you?"

"Hello, Jo dear. How you doing? Got over that hangover of yours yet?" she laughed.

"Yes, yes, thanks. I have." Phew, I thought. No sign of any change. I carried on.

"I was just wondering what we needed for Thursday's class? My email's playing up so I haven't got Helena's list."

"Oh, right," said Beryl. "That's a bit of a bugger, well this week we are doing a formal centre piece using dandelions. I'm sure Helena's been at the bottle before she comes up with these ideas, you'd have to be well on your way to think of that one, now wouldn't you?"

"Yes, I suspect you're right," I said.

I took a deep breath.

"Beryl, is Bill about?" I hoped she didn't sense the tension in my voice.

"No love, he's not, he's down at market today, why?"

"Oh, it's nothing important." Think, think, I implored myself, come up with a reason to get his mobile number. Even I was impressed with the speed at which I came up with my excuse.

"Oh," I said nonchalantly. "It's just I remember him saying he knew someone who kept ponies down at Steppings Gill, I was wondering if he could give me the number?"

"Your Rebecca wanting to take up riding then is she? Expensive hobby you know, Jo?"

"Yes, I know, it's George's idea. Thinks it will be good for her socially."

"Well, he won't be back till late, but you can ring him on his mobile if you like?"

"Thanks that would be great." Result! I was so relieved; perhaps I'm getting better at this lying thing after all.

She gave me the number.

"Right then, I guess I'll see you Thursday," I said.

"You will, indeed, don't forget your dandelions will you."

"No, I won't. Bye Beryl."

"Bye love."

Done, I put the phone down with a huge sigh of relief. I was surprised at how easy it had been. But then why wouldn't it be, she trusted me.

Coffee and my secret cig were called for. Ringing Bill would not be easy.

I retreated to the back of the greenhouse and went over what I would say to him. Another deep breath and I went back into the house and dialled his number.

"Hello, Bill South."

"Hi Bill," I said nervously. "It's Jo." There was a moment's silence.

"Oh, hello Jo. What can I do for you?" Bad choice of words Bill, I could hear the caution in his voice.

"I... I need to talk to you," I stammered. "About the other night, but not on the phone, please can we meet up somewhere?"

"Err, I'm not sure that's such a good idea Jo. I think perhaps it would be best to leave things as they are don't you?" He sounded worried.

"Please Bill, I promise I just want to talk; I need to get some things straight in my head that's all."

There was silence.

"Bill, Bill, you still there?"

His voice came back, calm and firm.

"OK, I'll be going for lunch at about 1.00pm at the Woolly Sheep in town, can you meet me there?"

"Yes, yes, that's fine. Thank you."

"OK. See you then. Bye." He put the phone down.

Bill, I could tell, was as unsettled about what had happened as I was.

I got ready, possibly taking a little more time with my appearance than was appropriate, given the circumstances, but I wanted to look nice for him. I didn't want him to see me and think, *bloody hell I'm glad it was dark.*

I needed to go to the library before I went into town. Vera and I had developed a sort of regular slot on a Monday and Thursday. I contemplated whether I should tell her what had happened over the weekend and decided it was best not to.

Vera was busy dusting shelves when I walked in and Fred Emmerson had already arrived.

"Morning, Fred." I said cheerily.

"Morning, Anne." He had a different name for me each time I went in, if he was there.

"Morning, Vera, shall I put the kettle on?" I peeked behind the shelf.

"Oh, hello there Jo, nice to see ya love, yes please I'm dying for a cuppa."

I went into the little kitchen and made the tea. A few moments later Vera followed me in.

"So, then," she said, "how did it go on Friday?" she had a mischievous glint in her eye, "I hope you didn't do anything I wouldn't do." She nudged me in the side.

"To be honest Vera, that gives me an awful lot of scope, now doesn't it?"

"What are you trying to say, young whippersnapper? I hope you're not casting aspersions as to my good character."

"Now would I? Tea?" I carried the tray through to the desk and we both sat down. I'd made an extra cup for Fred.

"But you had a good time, though, yeah?" she said.

"I did," I replied, "but I'm afraid to say I did have rather too much to drink. I ended up staying at Beryl and Bill's."

"Did you now?" There seemed to be a knowing tone in her voice. Oh great, this is where I find out they've got a reputation for this sort of thing. Luring unsuspecting drunken women back to the house so Bill can seduce them. I tried not to register any kind of reaction.

"I bet that went down well with George."

Phew, she meant something different. God this was hard.

"Well, he wasn't thrilled about it, but you were so right about standing up to him. Besides, he's not exactly squeaky clean himself at the moment."

I went on to tell her about finding the hotel bill and the receipts for the lingerie.

"The sneaky bugger, no wonder he doesn't want you going out, he's worried you'll catch him out."

"I know, that's what I thought."

"So what are you going to do?"

"I'm not sure yet, it's a tricky one because of Rebecca."

I told her about what had happened on the Sunday morning and my fears that George might have left me.

"Nah," she said, "for all his faults and from what you've told me, he loves Rebecca. He's not going to do anything that will hurt her. He's cooling off that's all, happen he knows you're on to him and he's just taking some time out. He'll be back, mark my words."

"Do you think so?"

"I do love, you just wait and see." She gave my hand a reassuring pat.

I placed my hand on top of hers and gave it a squeeze.

"I owe you so much Vera; you have been so kind to me. I know we haven't known each other for very long, but I just want you to know how much I value your friendship. I just wish there was something I could do to say thank you."

"Oh, now give up ya soppy cow, I don't need any thanks."

"Well, at least let me take you out or something. I know, how about we go out for a proper girlie lunch one day this week? We could go to that posh place just down the road."

"You don't need to do that."

"Please, I'd like to."

"Well, if you insist, that would be lovely."

"What day shall we say then, how about Thursday after flower class?"

"Yes, I can do that. Don't suppose you're free this afternoon are you?"

"'Fraid not, sorry I have to go into town, why?"

"Oh, nothing important, I'd planned to go to Leeds to do a bit of shopping, that's all. I just quite fancied the company."

"Why on earth would you want to go to Leeds, Vera? I can't think of anything worse!"

"Oh, I love it." she said. "I like the bustle and the shops. It's all so much more interesting than round here."

"I could go another day with you."

"No, no, it's fine, if you're not keen, no point in you going just for my sake."

"Well, if you're sure, you will be all right on your own though won't you?"

"'Course I bloody will you cheeky minx, I do it all the time."

"Well," I said, standing up. "I'm sorry to love you and leave you, but I must get going, I'll come and pick you up on Thursday at about half twelve, yeah?" I reached over and gave her a hug and a kiss on the cheek.

"Right you are, love. I'll look forward to it. Bye."

I left the library, drove to town and got to the pub at about five past one.

I felt nervous as I pushed the door open; I never had been comfortable going into places on my own. I always felt as though people were looking at me. George used to say I was stupid to think that.

"Why on earth would anyone be looking at you, Marjorie?" he would mock, "It's not like you're anything special."

Thankfully, it was quiet and I immediately spotted Bill sat in a corner. He stood up and waved. I went over and sat down.

"Hi Jo, How are you?" He said politely. I could tell he was nervous. His eyes kept darting round the room to see if anyone had spotted us.

"I'm fine," I said.

"I'll get you a drink shall I?" He stood up too quickly and knocked his pint, spilling a little on the table. He was definitely uneasy.

"What would you like, do you want something to eat, they do a good lunch menu here, the meat and potato pie is very tasty, or you could...."

I put my hand on his hand to calm him. "Just a mineral water, thanks," I said.

I watched him as he went to the bar. Poor man, God knows what terrible thoughts were running through his head. He came back with the drinks and sat down.

"It's kind of you to agree to see me," I said. "I know how difficult this must be for you."

"I just don't want anything to hurt our Beryl." His voice was quiet and earnest. "I couldn't believe it when I realised she'd forgotten what she said. I only did what I did because I thought she was OK with it."

"I know, I feel just the same way. That's why I wanted to see you, find out what had happened."

"Well, she was obviously a lot drunker than I'd realised. She can't remember anything past coming home from the pub. I'm going to stop making that bloody plum brandy." He took a large slug of his pint.

"And if she had remembered?" I questioned. "Would she genuinely have been OK with it? I know I wouldn't be."

He went quiet for a moment.

"Yes, yes she would," he said softly but definitely.

"Well then, she's one unusual woman!"

"Yes, she is, more unusual that you could possibly imagine."

He paused and looked at me; I could tell he was considering whether he should share what he was thinking. He took a deep breath.

"There's something that I think you should know about me and Beryl, Jo. It might help you to understand things a bit better."

Oh my God, what's he going to tell me? That Beryl's a man waiting for the op and that's why Bill was allowed to play with other women?

No, it couldn't be, her chest was far too big. No one would deliberately get boobs that big, well not unless they were in the porn industry anyway.

Bloody hell, that's it. They're porn stars. I bet they filmed the whole thing. Oh my God, I'm destined to be the next internet sex tape sensation; George would definitely leave me now. The shame of it, I'll never be able to show my face at flower club again!

My new found ability to run away with the fairies was quite impressive; I seemed to be able to conjure up the most ridiculous scenarios in a matter of seconds. I reined my head in and told myself, none of these could be true. No, the explanation for their liberated attitude must be something far more straightforward. I was almost sitting on the edge of my seat in anticipation.

He spoke slowly and carefully, "What happened on Friday was not so unusual for me and Beryl." There was another slight pause. "It's happened before."

My face must have registered my shock, even though I was trying to be extraordinarily cool about the whole thing.

He carried on.

"I don't mean we make a habit of inviting women round to the house so I can have my wicked way with them, but the idea of having different partners to each other, well it's not new to us. You see years ago when we were younger, we were very into swinging."

"Swinging!" I said, astonished. "You mean the whole car keys in the fruit bowl business?" I was completely taken aback but it certainly explained a lot.

"Yes," he continued. "I mean going to parties where you swap partners and have sex with them. Beryl has always been

89

the more adventurous one out of the two of us, she has, well how can I put it...?"

"The sex drive of a bitch on heat perhaps?"

"Well, let's just say her sex drive is very high. Or it used to be, seems to be calming down a bit now she's getting older but she's still pretty demanding."

"I see," I said.

"Beryl was the one that wanted to try the swinging thing, I went along with it, well, because, I didn't want to disappoint her. Don't get me wrong, I wasn't forced to do it, sometimes I did enjoy it. But truth be told, I am a one woman man. I didn't need the same kind of excitement as her, she was always enough for me. But she likes the thrill you see, the adventure of being with someone different. In the end, I agreed that she could carry on going to these parties and that I would stay at home. As long as she didn't tell me anything about it, I was OK with it."

"That's extraordinarily understanding of you Bill," I said.

"I know." He looked sad and somehow forlorn.

"Thing is you see Jo, I love her, I love the very bones of her and I want her to be happy. She just does it once in a while now which is easier for me, but she does still get the urge and well... I have to let her go."

I was amazed that he genuinely believed his wife could only be happy if she slept with other men. It would emotionally confuse the hell out of me.

He carried on.

"The way I see it is this: if I said no and got all stroppy about it, she'd still have these urges and end up at it with someone behind my back. If I let her indulge her fantasy life a bit, I know she'll always come back to me because she always has. It was certainly a gamble in the early days, but now she has her flings at these parties and she comes home. She's never had an affair and I know deep down that she loves me.

I honestly think she can't help herself; I know she feels guilty about it sometimes. I think that's what all this business was about on Friday night. I think she thought if I had a bit of hanky-panky with you it would kind of balance things out a bit."

He paused and took another drink, obviously considering what to say next.

"You must understand Jo, she's not a bad person. She just has needs, needs that can't be fulfilled by just being with me."

The woman's off her head. If I had access to that kind of pleasure every day, you'd never get me out of bed.

He continued, "So if you're hoping that I'll leave her or that you and I can have some kind of affair, then I'm sorry, but as kind an offer as it may be, I'd have to say no."

His loyalty was astonishing; he was either the loveliest, most understanding man on the planet or seriously in need of growing a pair. I liked to think it was the former.

"Bill," I said calmly, "I promise you, I did not come here today to beg you to have an affair with me. I just wanted to make sure that we were OK, and that you agree not telling Beryl was the right thing to do. I would hate there to be any awkwardness between us. You and Beryl are two of the only friends I've got and I don't want to spoil that for the sake of a drunken indiscretion. If you're happy to move on and forget about it, then I certainly am. OK?"

"Sounds good to me," he said. "Not that I didn't enjoy the other night, because I did, it's just..."

"It's fine," I said. "Let's just leave it at that, shall we?"

I could visibly see the relief on his face. "Yes, yes, that would suit me just fine. Just one thing though, Jo. No one except Jean knows about this and she's been cool with it for years. It's not something I want the whole village talking about, so I would appreciate if you didn't say anything to anyone."

"Of course not Bill," I reassured. "I wouldn't dream of it."

I stood up to go.

"Well, thanks for your time Bill, it was much appreciated."

He leaned forward, took my hand and gave me a kiss on the cheek. I could smell his aftershave and a rush of memories from Friday night came flooding back. I breathed the scent of him in, allowing it to trigger the sensations that I had felt just a few days before. God, I wish I could have one more session with him.

He let go of my hand.

I drove home feeling relieved that I had cleared the air with Bill, but feeling uncertain about where my feelings lay for Beryl.

Here was a woman that I had instantly warmed to, that had shown me friendship and compassion in a way I had never known before. Yet her behaviour as far as my under-standing of relationships was concerned was totally appalling and completely alien to me.

How could she do what she does and carry on a normal life?

I resolved that essentially I had no right to judge her. After all, somewhere in my uptight sense of morality I was a brazen and abandoned hussy, ready to hurl myself at the first male to offer me some attention. I had allowed her husband to seduce me. Admittedly, I was several glasses of wine and plum brandy worse for wear, but that can't be an excuse, can it?

Don't 'they' say that you're more your true self when you're drunk? That your inhibitions are curbed and you do all the things you would like to do, but would never dare to when you are sober. If that was the case, then was my behaviour any better than Beryl's? If my first foray into the social world after so long had led to this outburst of wanton sexual desire, perhaps I was more like her than I realised. Perhaps I should have a go at this swinging malarkey then – I wonder, do they accept single, married ladies or is it just couples?

I doubted I would ever find out, It's not like I could ask Beryl. She would want to know how I knew about her extra-curricular activities. Then the whole story about meeting Bill would come out and that would be it.

No, accept her for who she is, I told myself, and just hope your Rampant Rabbit has arrived!

9

Terrible News

It got to Wednesday before I realised George hadn't been in touch. He usually rang me from his hotel every couple of days and although our conversations were always brief, he did have long chats with Rebecca.

Regardless of what was going on between us, I couldn't believe he wouldn't still want to speak to his daughter. I found myself considering the possibility that something might have happened to him.

I went through all the scenarios: accidents, plane crashes even murder. The most awful thing was, I realised my panic and worry was not because I feared losing George, I feared losing my security.

What if he's changed his will, this unknown bimbo he's been cavorting with is going to get my home. My life as I knew it was hanging in the balance, I would have nowhere to go, no income, and no roof over my head. Bloody hell Marjorie, how could you allow yourself to become so vulnerable?

My conclusion – if George's demise just conjured a feeling of panic as to where I would live, then I needed to accept this marriage was over and make sure I was not left high and dry.

My concerns for George's welfare were of course unfounded. I found out over dinner that he had been ringing Rebecca every night on her mobile to make sure she was OK.

The sneaky bugger, how dare he go behind my back? But at the same time, at least he's been in touch with her.

Rebecca could tell I was not happy.

"I'm sorry Mum," she said. "I thought you knew. I didn't mean to upset you." She was genuinely concerned.

"It's OK Rebecca," I reassured. "Really, don't worry about it. It's not your fault, I'm glad your dad has been ringing you."

"Mum," she said slowly. "Is everything OK with you and Dad?"

What should I say? Should I tell her the truth? Break the bubble of her believing that her father was the most wonderful person in the world. Or just stay quiet until I had a better idea of what was going to happen.

"Everything is fine darling," I lied. "Now why don't you go and finish your homework? I'll bring you some hot chocolate up in a bit."

She came and gave me a kiss and wandered off to her bedroom. Within a few minutes I could hear the ghastly noise of whatever new band she was into and I knew she was fine.

I sat and pondered.

It was beginning to feel more and more as though George did have a game plan. I'd never seriously considered that before. There I was sat with my coffee, contemplating the outcome of my life; knowing that I had entrusted it to a man who for all I knew was holed up in a hotel somewhere, doing God knows what to God knows who.

Was he biding his time? Was he getting his ducks in a row before he let out the fatal shot?

I started to think about Rebecca. How would she deal with it? True to say if George left it wouldn't make that much difference to her day to day routines, he was so rarely here anyway. He might be a crap husband, but he was a good dad so I knew he would make sure her life was left as undamaged as possible. This would hopefully mean I would get to keep the house, at least for the next few years anyway.

But what of this 'other woman'? I might not care or have any feeling regarding George's infidelity, but the idea of

Rebecca meeting this person and having some kind of relationship with her was totally unacceptable to me. I was just starting to get my little girl back, I'd be dammed if this woman was going to jeopardise that. Friday, I decided; if I hadn't heard from him by then, I would try and get hold of him.

My thoughts were broken and I physically jumped when the phone rang.

I half expected it to be George and I got nervous butterflies in my stomach as I picked up, but it wasn't George, it was Beryl.

God, will I ever be able to speak to this woman without always thinking she knows about me and her husband?

"Hi Beryl, how are you?"

"Oh Jo, I'm sorry to bother you so late love, but I thought I'd better ring you before tomorrow and tell you. I'm sorry, but I've got some terrible news."

My heart leapt into my mouth and thoughts raced as to what she could mean. Beryl was not one for over reacting so if she said something was bad, you could be pretty sure it was.

My first thought, of course, was that it was something to do with George.

"What is it Beryl, what's happened?" I urged.

"It's Vera, Jo. Vera from the library."

Thank God I thought, it's just Vera.

"Oh phew, Beryl, I thought it was something serious, for a moment you had me worried."

"No Jo, let me finish, God, I don't know how to tell you. There's been..." She was struggling to get her words out, "there's been an awful accident."

"Accident? Oh no, I bet she's fallen down those bloody steps at the library hasn't she? I kept telling her they needed to put a ramp in. Which hospital is she in, has anyone been to see her yet?"

"No Jo," Beryl implored, "please listen to me, she's not in the hospital." Another pause, "She's, she's – dead."

"Dead?" I said in disbelief. "Dead! She can't be."

"I'm so, so sorry love, I know you two were close."

I sat down in shock. Close, we were more than close; this woman had changed my life. She had become my confidante, a dear, dear friend. I knew she was well passed her sell by date, but I never considered that she would die. I'd always imagined her just slowly disintegrating in a corner of the library and becoming part of the dust on the shelves. How could she be dead? How could life be so cruel and take this person from me so soon after she had become such a wonderful part of my life? I was truly stunned.

"Oh my God," I gasped. "I can't take this in. W...what happened, I only saw her on Monday? She was fine. She'd just booked her next holiday. She was going trekking in Tibet in July. I just can't believe it!"

"I know," said Beryl. "I can't take it in either."

"Do we know how? It's not like she was ill or anything."

"Well, that's the worst of it you see love. It's not like she just dropped down dead or anything. It was the mugging that did it."

"Mugging!" I exclaimed. "What mugging? How the hell could she get mugged in the library? We don't do mugging round here do we?"

"No, no, not here," she reassured. "She'd gone to Leeds for the day shopping. Ended up at the far end of town where all the crafty type shops and stuff are. You know what she was like, always into her 'alternative' stuff. Seems some young girl took a fancy to her handbag and tried to snatch it. Course Vera, being Vera, she wasn't going to give it up without a fight so she struggled with this lass and ended up getting hit and pushed to the ground. The girl ran off without getting anything, but poor old Vera's heart just couldn't stand the excitement. She had a heart attack. They took her to the hospital, but she didn't last the night, poor old gal."

"That's appalling," I said. "Poor Vera, I don't know what to say."

Beryl carried on, "Caught the little bitch that did it though, some passer-by grabbed her and God love him, he wasn't letting go for love nor money."

"Well, I suppose that's something."

"I'm sorry to be the bearer of such bad news, Jo. I rang as soon as I'd heard; I knew you would want to know. They're having the funeral at St. Margaret's next Monday, no flowers just donations to the Tibetan Freedom Fighters' Fund. Although, she did say if the flower club wanted to come up with something inappropriate they could, as long as no one spent any money. Thought we could have a chat about it tomorrow see what we can do, eh?"

"Yes, yes, sure, of course." I was still in complete shock. "Well, thanks for letting me know Beryl."

"That's all right love." She paused before saying, "Makes you realise how precious people are don't it?"

"Yes, yes, I suppose it does," I replied. "I'll see you tomorrow, bye."

"Night night love, hope you get some sleep."

I put the phone down and Rebecca rushed into the hall to see what was wrong. She must have heard me from upstairs.

"What is it Mummy, what's happened you look terrible, it's not Daddy is it, has something happened to him?" She grabbed my hand and I could see she was getting upset.

I stood up and put my arms around her. "Shh, no Becca, it's not Daddy, he's fine. No, it's Vera, Vera from the library. She's had a terrible accident and well, very sadly she's died." I couldn't stop myself I just burst into tears.

"Oh no. Mummy that's so awful, she was such a lovely lady."

"Yes, yes, I know, I know," I snivelled. "She was a very special person I'm going to really miss her."

Poor Rebecca, I don't think she had ever seen me cry before and she had no idea how to react.

"I'm sorry darling, it was just rather a shock, I'm fine, honestly, please don't be worried."

"It's OK Mum, I understand." She stood looking at me then unexpectedly said, "I know, let me go and make you a nice cup of tea."

She disappeared into the kitchen.

Crikey, where on earth did that come from? I wiped my tears away, blew my nose and took a deep breath.

"Bloody hell, Rebecca," I shouted. "Do you actually know where the kettle is?"

"Oi!" she retorted. "Don't be so ungrateful and err, less of the swearing thank you mother."

She made me a cup of tea and we spent the rest of the evening sitting in the kitchen swapping stories about Vera. I hadn't felt this close to her since she was a little girl. It was lovely.

I shed a few more tears and then finally went up to bed with heavy gritty eyes feeling empty.

Flower club the next day was rightly very sombre. Our dandelion centrepieces had been postponed in preference to discussions on what to make for the funeral on Monday.

I also learned a little more about what had happened on that fateful day. Jean's husband, being the local doctor, was very well in with the police and he had managed to get us a lot more detail.

It seems the girl that attacked Vera was in her early twenties and had, as I could have guessed, a drink and drugs problem. This was by all accounts her first offence, so the likelihood was she would be charged with aggravated assault but not manslaughter. Her case was due to be heard at Leeds

Crown Court in a couple of weeks. She hadn't even been remanded, but had got bail on condition that her parents were responsible for her until the hearing.

"It's a bloody disgrace!" Beryl said. "Evil cow should be given life for what she's done."

"I know, I know," said Jean, "but it's not likely, she'll probably get probation and a bit of community service. This is what happens: when they have 'problems' the courts go easy on them, try and get them rehabilitated rather than locking them up. They just don't have the resources nowadays to deal with the number of petty criminals that operate out there. I'm not saying it's right, just likely as not that's how it'll end up."

"Beryl's right," I piped up. "It is a bloody disgrace, how dare this girl think she can get away with it? Nobody forced her to pour drink and drugs down her neck, but it's all right for people like poor Vera to pay the price for her not being able to get a fucking grip.

We all have problems, but we don't go round blaming other people for our own stupidity. Why should this girl be any different to the rest of us? The last time I heard, knocking down old ladies and trying to steal their handbags was still classed as breaking the law. You know full well that it's wrong and if you get caught you should get punished. Otherwise, what's the bloody point of having laws and courts and judges?

What kind of message are we sending our kids if every time someone commits a crime, some pubescent graduate social worker sticks their two penneth in and says; 'Oh your honour, it wasn't their fault, they have had a terrible time of it! Their benefits just don't cover the amount of cash they need to pay for their daily drug and drink requirements'. Makes me sick!"

I was so angry and my words so venomous, there was a moment's silence when I had finished.

"Steady on Jo, you'll do yourself a mischief carrying on like that." Beryl was trying to calm me down. "There's

100

nothing we can do about it. If she does get away with it, ranting and carrying on won't help any of us, now will it?"

"She's right, Jo," said Jean. "We're all as angry as you, but there is nothing anyone can do."

Despite their attempts to placate me, I was still seething. Not just because one of my best friends had been taken from me, but because it seemed likely that the person who had caused all this pain was pretty much going to get away with it. It was just wrong, morally wrong.

"Well," I said. "It's just not good enough, you lot may be happy to just sit and see justice not be done. But I'll be damned if I will."

"Oh, now come on, Jo," retorted Jean. "If there was anything we could do, you know we would. But there just isn't."

"Well, I can at least try," I said. "I'm not just going to sit back and do nothing!"

We left the conversation there and parted a very low and dejected bunch. The only slight lift to our spirits was reaching agreement on what arrangement we should make for Vera's funeral.

We all concluded that the most fitting tribute to our wonderful friend was a giant wild flower teapot. This was to represent the hundreds of cups of tea she had made for anyone who had passed through the doors of her beloved library.

I arrived home, having almost forgotten that as well as dealing with the horror of Vera's death, I still had my own drama to contend with in the guise of the wonderful wandering George. Talk about putting things into perspective; George's affair and my fears that he would leave me just didn't seem that important any more.

It got to Friday night and I was just beginning to think about calling him, when the phone rang.

"Marjorie. It's George." I recognised the tone of his voice; it was the one he used if I was in trouble. It reminded me of a strict school teacher about to deliver a lecture on why snogging behind the bike sheds was inappropriate.

"Well, hello stranger." I deliberately made my tone contrast to his by sounding trite and light, "I was beginning to wonder what had happened to you. Thought perhaps Belgium had been subject to a military coup and you were holed up in the British Embassy, waiting for the SAS to airlift you out? Funny though, there's nothing on the news about it."

I knew this would wind him up, but confess the level of his anger did surprise me.

"Don't be so ridiculous, woman!" he barked. "Why do you have to be so bloody stupid all the time? I don't know what's come over you lately Marjorie but I'll tell you one thing I'm not going to stand for it. Christ, I swear your grasp on reality is getting worse by the day!"

Bit harsh of him, but I knew exactly what he was doing. He will have spent at least an hour trying to pluck up the courage to make the call. Me being all light and fluffy will just make him feel even more of a shit than he already was. His reaction was pure guilt. Making me out to be at fault was his way of alleviating his feelings of being a complete and utter dick.

"Oh for goodness sake George, lighten up will you?" I laughed, "I was joking and please, you have no need to be concerned about my grasp on reality. I can assure you, it's tighter than it has ever been."

"Yes. Well," he huffed. "Not funny, Marjorie, not funny at all."

God, how could I never have realised? He has absolutely no sense of humour. What on earth does Miss Push-Up Babydoll see in him? Or perhaps it was just the effect I had on him. Perhaps I had sucked the life blood out of this man by being so dull and boring for so many years.

I had made him so miserable his sole comfort was clandestine meetings with woman who wore bustiers and crotchless knickers. Perhaps when he was away from me he was a sexy cad about town thrilling all the ladies with his witty repartee.

He's going to tell me; he's going to come clean.

"Sorry George," I said softly. "Can we expect you home any time?"

"I'm coming home tomorrow," was his curt response. "We need to talk Marjorie; there are things that we need to sort out."

"OK," I said, "are you still in Belgium, then? What time does your flight get in?"

There was a slight pause. "No, I'm not in Belgium, I'm back in the UK. I'll be over first thing in the morning, no later than about 9.30am."

A-ha, I realised, he's close by then.

"Right," I said, sounding puzzled. "So you're in the UK but you're not coming home tonight. So where are you George?"

"My flight got in late, so I decided to stay in town." He was sounding defensive.

I bet you did, no doubt about to embark on a session with your little tart. I decided not to push things any further. Having a full blown row over the phone was not the most sensible thing to do. It's not like he's going to tell me something I didn't already know. No, let him have tonight to get his head together.

"Ah, I see," I said. "That's fine. That'll work out quite well, Rebecca's at a friend's tonight. She's not due back until tomorrow afternoon. We can have a nice long chat, without having to worry about her overhearing. But I'm guessing you already knew that, didn't you George?"

His voice was quiet in its reply, "Yes, yes, I did," he said.

"Right, well, tomorrow at 9.30 it is then. Night, George. Don't stay up too late. You know how grouchy you are if you don't get enough sleep."

I could almost hear the cogs turning as he pondered whether I knew what he was up to, cruel of me really. I just couldn't help enjoying the sense of power this knowledge gave me. Yes, it would be short lived, but what the hell; I could have a few moments of getting my own back couldn't I? I left a brief silence and then put the phone down and considered the rest of the evening.

It was quite late and I decided going to bed was the best idea. I grabbed my cigarettes, a glass of wine and the rather discreetly wrapped box that had arrived for me in the post and headed up stairs.

10
Life is a Cabaret

I woke on Saturday morning and for a brief moment forgot what lay in store.

I had a gloriously indulgent hour before I fell asleep, playing with my new toy whilst imagining the wonderful caresses of my forbidden Bill.

I can't think why women bother with men any more. These gadgets are far more sophisticated than your average male member and you certainly never have to fake an orgasm with them, or placate their egos by telling them how wonderful they are in bed. Oh yes, I was a definite convert to that particular naughty habit.

I had further indulged my new found debauchery by allowing myself a cigarette in the house.

"No one's here except me," I said to myself. "Why the hell shouldn't I? I'm in my own room."

The cigarettes, the wine and the thoughts of my illicit fantasy had nicely blocked out the dreadfulness of the previous few days, and I had slept well.

I got up and dressed, yet again deciding to take more time than I usually would.

I had been doing quite well at the gym and was definitely a lot more toned than before. I'd even bought new clothes, not that George would notice, but then that wasn't the point was it? If this man was going to walk in and tell me how inadequate I was as his wife, I was damn well going to make sure I looked as good as I could whilst he did it.

I put on for me, what was quite a provocative dress; a little lower cut than I would perhaps normally wear and slightly shorter in length. I did my hair and makeup and went downstairs.

I was unexpectedly nervous waiting for him to arrive. My usual feelings of contempt had been replaced by anxious anticipation, you might even call it excitement and I was annoyed at myself for feeling anything at all.

His car pulled into the drive bang on 9.30am. Punctual as ever George, I thought. I watched as he got out of the car, he looked tired, and dishevelled. His suit looked as though he had slept in it and he had obviously rushed his morning shave. Well, I decided, your new woman clearly is a new woman. Apparently she doesn't believe in the use of an iron, or in sleep by the look of him. Poor George, I think he may be out of his depth with this one.

He began to walk up the steps.

"Hello George," I said, leaning nonchalantly with my arm up on the edge of the door. That pose always looked so good in films. "Do come in. Can I get you some coffee?"

"Morning Marjorie." His voice was low and gruff and he didn't even look up as he walked in, "Yes, please." He headed straight for the sitting room, a huge sigh followed as he plonked himself on the cushions.

I made the coffee and took the tray through and sat on the opposite sofa.

"I have to say George, you look like shit."

I waited expectantly for his curt response to my 'bad' language, but it never came.

"Do I?" he said. "I suppose I do." He took a sip of his coffee.

I must admit this was not the George I had expected to see.

From his conversation on the phone, I had imagined he would arrive with a clipboard and agenda ready to chair the meeting.

"So George," I said eventually, after quite a long awkward silence. "You wanted to talk to me about something?"

"Yes," he said, "I do, I'm just not sure how to start." His voice was soft, almost dejected. I had never seen him look so helpless.

Here we go, self-pity abounding. "I'm listening," I said.

He took another sip of coffee.

"You have to realise Marjorie, when I spoke to you last night, things were different. I was very sure of what needed to be done and knew exactly what needed to be said; but then during the course of the evening things changed and I'm afraid I'm not quite sure where I am with this situation anymore."

She's dumped him, I surmised, that's why he's looking the way he is. He's made all these plans to leave me and set up his little love nest with her and right at the last minute she's given him the elbow. Brilliant, bloody brilliant, that scenario hadn't even crossed my mind. Now he's had to come home, aware deep down that I know what he's been doing. Knowing that he's still going to have to come clean, beg my forgiveness and hope I'll take him back. Ha, now that's Karma!

"This is so hard for me," he said. He took another sip of his coffee.

Hard for him, hard for him, how dare he? Don't you expect any sympathy from me George Primm, not after what you've been up to!

"I'm sorry," he said. "I know this last week must have been difficult for you too, and I do realise you know something has been going on."

"You're damn right there," I snarled.

"Before this gets nasty, I just want to say thank you. Thank you for behaving in a dignified and decent way. You could very easily have made things a lot harder for me and I just want you to know that it is appreciated."

"OK," I said. "Just cut to the chase will you, George? I do think you owe me the courtesy of an explanation, don't you?"

He looked troubled and pensive as he spoke.

"Yes, yes of course I do, but if you could just give me a little time there are some things I must tell to you that go back way beyond last week. There are things you don't know about me Marjorie and I'm not sure how you're going to take what I have to tell you."

"This is all sounding very odd George. You're not in trouble with the police or anything are you?"

I had the most dreadful thought. "Oh my god, it's not an affair is it? It's prostitutes!" I blurted. "You've been caught kerb crawling, haven't you? I should have guessed. Of course, that's it. It's always the ones that make high moral judgements on everyone else that are up to the dirtiest things behind closed doors."

My mind began working its usual fateful overtime.

"Jesus, I bet it ends up in the papers. Oh no, what about Rebecca? She'll get bullied at school, and we'll be the laughing stock of the whole area! Well, there's only one thing for it, we're going to have to move and just when I'd started to like living round here as well. George, how could you? Well, all I can say is thank God we don't sleep together any more. God knows what I could have caught from you."

"For crying out loud woman, would you listen to yourself?" he shouted.

He was starting to get angry. He stood up violently and for a moment I seriously believed he was going to lash out and hit me. I instinctively raised my arm up to protect myself. But he didn't, he paced over to the window.

"You're at it again, rambling on making assumptions about who people are and what they are doing. It's nothing like that; I would never do anything like that. My God, doesn't that just say it all? Shows us just how little we truly know each other."

He sat down and put his head to his hands, brushing his hair back and then resting his elbows on his knees.

"I wouldn't need to make assumptions if you talked to me occasionally," I barked. "What else am I supposed to think? You leave me here for days at a time, I never know when or if you're coming home and when you are here you treat me like shit. I spend most of my life thinking I'm sodding invisible. Is it any wonder I go off on flights of fantasy, it's the only life I have!"

"Look," he said calmly, "I don't want this to turn into a screaming match. I know, I don't deserve your patience or understanding; but if you could just let me say what I need to say, I would be most grateful."

"Go on then," I said sarcastically. "I'm all ears."

He took another sip of coffee.

"It may come as a surprise to you Marjorie, but I do know that I have not been a very good husband. Yes, I provide for you and I look after your day to day needs, but I have never been a true companion or lover to you and the awful truth is I knew I never could be. Even on the day I married you I knew deep down that I would never make you happy."

"What?" I said dubiously. "What the hell do you mean George?"

He continued, "All these years we have spent together Marjorie, they are such a waste; a waste of two lives, two people that could have been so much more than they have been by being together. You, you could have been anything you wanted, but instead you married me and gave up your life to live a lie you didn't even know you were living."

109

"OK George, now this is just a little bit too much for even me to grasp. Are you having a breakdown or something? Is it time for your mid-life crisis, because to be honest, I thought we'd passed that one about ten years ago."

He came over and sat beside me on the sofa and took my hand. He was beginning to make me feel nervous. I had never heard him talk like this. It was totally out of character for him. This man was not my husband.

"Whoa," I said. "Stop right there, have you had a bang on the head or something? George this just isn't you; I don't know what you've done with the real one but bring him back right now! Please, this is seriously starting to freak me out."

"It's OK, Marjorie," he was trying to be reassuring. "Really, I'm not having a breakdown, well not in the way you think anyway. Believe it or not, I am for once in my ridiculous lie of a life, trying to do the right thing."

He looked me in the eyes. "I'm sorry Marjorie but I have to say something and it's going to hurt you. I don't want it to, but I think you deserve to know the truth."

"Bloody hell George, talk about drama." I snatched my hand out of his. "What on earth are you going on about? Are you still drunk or something? For God's sake drink some more of that coffee, will you?"

"Marjorie, please." He was shouting again.

He stood up sharply and turned round to face me. He wasn't angry he was upset, I could see the tears in his eyes.

"This is hard enough; please don't make it any harder. What I'm trying to tell you, Oh God, I am so sorry, but the truth is, the truth is..."

My patience was wearing thin. "Oh for crying out loud, spit it out will you? Oh God I'll say it, then shall I... you're having an affair, I already know!"

"No, no, it's not that," he said, "what I am trying to say is..." He paused. "I have never truly loved you, Marjorie." He blurted the words out in a fast stream as though by saying them quickly he could forget that he had said them at all. He flopped back down on the sofa repeating the words again quietly.

"I have never loved you... and I married you knowing that."

"I beg your pardon!" I shouted, standing up. I was astounded. I didn't quite know why, but tears welled up in my eyes; I was trying to fight them back but it was just such a shock. So if he wasn't having an affair, what the hell was going on? All my bravado disappeared, I felt as though someone had slugged me with a hammer.

He came and stood in front of me, resting his hands on both my shoulders.

"Don't you dare touch me," I snapped. "You are a bastard George, a complete and utter bastard! What the hell do you think you're playing at? How dare you say that to me after everything I have done to for you?"

I went and sat back down. My hands were shaking and I felt sick. I instinctively reached for my bag and took out my cigarettes. I saw him glance over.

"Don't even go there George," I snarled, "don't... even... go... there!"

He held up his hands. "It's OK," he said. "I understand. You go right ahead. But can I at least finish what I was going to say?"

I nodded. "Then you can pack up the rest of your things and get out!" I spat.

"I know what I said sounds harsh, but please, don't think I didn't care for you. I did and I do very, very much. I'm saying what I say not to hurt you, but to reassure you. I didn't want you blaming yourself for what has happened; I didn't want to put you through the torment of thinking that in some way you'd caused me to stop loving you. It would be totally wrong

111

of me to let you believe that my feelings for you have changed, if they were never there in the first place. Do you understand?"

"No George, I bloody don't," I snapped. "All I can see is that the last 15 years of my life have been a complete and utter lie. That everything I have given you and done for you has been wasted."

He came and sat beside me and put his arm around me.

"No they haven't," he said, "not completely. We might have screwed up our side of things, but don't forget we have a beautiful, intelligent daughter that's just beginning to blossom. She's something we can be proud of whatever else we've done. That's not a waste is it?"

"But I just don't get it," I snivelled. "Why did you marry me if you didn't love me? As I recall, it was you that did all the chasing, not me. If you hadn't pursued me so intently, I doubt I would have given you a second glance!"

"I know," he said. "I think looking back on it, I thought if I could get married and settle down I could change. That the person I was trying to escape being wouldn't follow me and I could have a normal life. I married you because I thought you would help me do that. I truly believed if I had a family I would be happy. After all, that's what everybody wants isn't it? For a long time it seemed to work, more so for me than for you I think, and I realise that now."

I sat dazed, feeling I was dreaming, none of this was making any sense.

He continued.

"It was as Rebecca got older that I realised one day I might have to face the truth. I knew you would start to question your life and what it meant. It was always my biggest fear. But I just wasn't ready to take that step, I was scared."

"Scared?" I retorted. "Scared of what? Just what are you hiding from George, what exactly is it you're so afraid to change? Are you telling me, that you prefer blondes to brunettes? Because we could have solved that one with a bottle of hair dye, my love."

"No Marjorie, I am not trying to tell you that I prefer blondes to brunettes; for someone that's very bright you can be extraordinarily thick sometimes. What I am trying to tell you in my own uptight, super controlled, never let anything show way, is that I prefer men to women."

I was lost for words. I sat, I am almost sure, un-originally open-mouthed.

"No!" I said in astonishment. "No, I'm not buying that one. You're trying to tell me you're gay? No George, not you, it just doesn't fit, no," I said firmly. "No, I'm sorry I just don't believe you, it's just an excuse to try and get away with having your bit on the side. I'll grant you, it's a bloody good one, but no, absolutely not."

"Marjorie," he looked me in the eye again. "It's true, I swear. I have spent most of my life denying it and I have finally decided that life is too short to fake. So, to coin a phrase, I've come out!"

"But you're just so... *not* gay," I protested. "You don't even like Barbara Streisand or Liza Minnelli. Or are you now going to confess that you have all their albums locked away in your study and you play them in secret when I've gone to bed?"

He laughed, "It isn't compulsory, you know. It's not like a club that you can't join unless you can recite the entire song repertoire from *Funny Girl* or *Cabaret*."

"OK," I said. "You win, I am totally and utterly confused, lost for words, don't know what to think. Why now George? Why now after all this time?"

"I'm not sure," he said. "It all came to a head, I think, the day you came back from your girls' night out."

He paused and took my hand again. "Oh Jo, you looked so different that day, so relaxed and at ease with yourself; you had a glow about you that I don't ever recall seeing before."

Oh shit, Can I visibly show I've had an orgasm, how amazingly inconvenient. I bet he's guessed, I bet he's guessed what I've done!

He continued, "I realised I could no longer keep the genie in the bottle. You were going to take your life back, and there was nothing I should do to stop you. I was amazed that you stuck things for as long as you did; I was always so afraid that you would go off and meet someone else. I think that's why I hated you going out because if you were always here, my life was always protected. I had tried for so long to guard myself, to keep the outward appearance going, but it was killing me inside and I hated myself for what I was doing to you. That's why I used to go away so much.

"When I saw you that day, I knew things were going to change; I had to get away. That's why I left so suddenly on the Sunday. I needed some time to decide if I really was brave enough to put the past behind me and give myself the chance to be the person I always should have been.

"When I spoke to you last night I had convinced myself that I couldn't go through with it. But then, I realised that no matter what I did, I was never going to change and to deny who I was, would just continue to destroy me and all the people I cared about. Life is just too short to piss about with and let's face it, we're not spring chickens anymore."

"Ahem, as I recall you were already a fully grown cock when we met! It's me that's had my youth robbed, thank you very much."

He laughed, "Well, however you see it, I didn't want us to spend the rest of our lives wishing that things had been different. If we'd carried on the way we were, we would have ended up despising each other and neither one of us deserves that. I accept full responsibility: it is totally my fault and I will

114

completely understand if you want to throw me out of the house and never see me again. The one thing I ask is **please**, please don't stop me seeing Rebecca?"

I looked at him closely; it was as though a different person had come into the room; his eyes seemed brighter and softer, his character so much more open.

I remembered the hotel bills.

"Err, hang on a minute," I said, "I found a hotel bill and a receipt for a load of lingerie in your trousers a few weeks back. How do you explain that, then?"

"Ah yes," he said. "Your famous digs about Malmaison. How could I forget? Well, yes, I have to confess you have me there. I have been having an affair, but it's not quite what you might think. My lover is a guy called Philip. He works as an accountant. In his spare time, however, he is known as Margo Marlene and is one of the headlining acts at the best drag club in Leeds. The lingerie was for his costumes which I bought him as a gift. The hotel was a special treat for his birthday."

"No," I said incredulously. "You're kidding, right? You're not seriously trying to tell me that not only have you come out of the closet, but you've come out of it in drag! This is just unbelievable, absolutely, totally unbe-fucking-leiveable. You could not make it up. If you stuck this in a soap they'd say it was too far-fetched! I have to hand it to you George. You don't do things by halves do you?"

"Rebecca, Jo, what about Rebecca?"

"Oh, I don't know George," I said dismissively. "Can you just give me a minute to let all this sink in? It's a hell of a bombshell you've just dropped."

"Yes, sorry, of course, take your time. Just for the record, though," he said timidly, "I don't dress up in drag, it's just Philip."

"Oh good, that makes everything so much better," I said sarcastically. "I'm going to make some more coffee."

I left him in the sitting room and went into the kitchen and lit another cigarette. It's emergency use only, that's all I told myself. I stood and looked out of the window whilst I waited for the kettle to boil. The same window I had watched from when George had driven off and I hadn't known if he was coming back. The whole thing just felt surreal. Could I believe him? Was this seriously the truth? It was a hell of a story to make up to cover your tracks if it wasn't.

I started to think about the past to see if there had been any clues; some sign that I could have picked up on that would have given him away.

The way he used to go clothes shopping with me was perhaps a little odd; but not an out and out indication that someone was gay, surely?

I hadn't ever considered him to be effeminate, quite the opposite. In fact, so much so that you might even think he was over compensating!

Bloody hell, I realised that's why he was such a male chauvinist pig. He didn't know how else to hide it. Going for that stereotype meant he could have kept it hidden forever. No one would bat an eye, it was absolute genius!

Then there was the sex. Now if ever there was a huge clue staring you in the face that was it. Yep, I really had been a bit of a dozy cow with that one. I had been so wrapped up in myself for so long, so deeply entrenched in my own belief that I was inadequate, it never occurred to me that anyone else could be at fault. If I had just been more confident, more willing to challenge him, this would have come to a head a hell of a lot sooner and saved an awful lot of heartache. George was right, it was a waste.

It's true that finding out your partner has been unfaithful carries all sorts of repercussions not easily dismissed. Jealousy, revenge, envy: all emotions that I had felt when I thought George was having an affair with another woman. But I just didn't feel any of them when thinking of him with another man.

I didn't feel angry anymore.

I had no reason to feel threatened by this. If anything, I was relieved, partly because things had come to a head and partly because it somehow vindicated me.

George was right to tell me he had never loved me; I did understand now.

I made the coffee and took it through to the sitting room.

George quickly hid what I could see was a mobile; he had obviously been texting Philip. No doubt to let him know how things were going.

"Well," I said. "Where do we go from here? Have you had any thoughts on what you want to do?"

"Not really," he said.

"To be honest, I had no idea how you would take it. For all I knew, I could have been lying on the kitchen floor with a carving knife in my back."

"Oh come, come George, you know I'm a pacifist; besides I'd never get the blood stains out of those tiles."

He smiled, "You know what I mean, it's not the kind of thing you can ever be prepared for is it? How are you feeling anyway?"

Wow, that's a first. George asking me how I feel!

"Surprisingly OK," I said. "It's funny, I actually feel quite calm. It's like all the pieces of a jigsaw have finally come together and the picture now makes sense."

"Yes, I know what you mean," he said. "I can't tell you how good it feels to tell you after so long."

"So have you had other affairs?" I asked. "Or is Philip the only one and how long have you been seeing him anyway?"

I was curious about the time frame to see if I could tie it in with any particular incidents between us.

117

"No, Philip is my first," he said. "Well, other than when I was much younger. Before I met you I mean and even those were not affairs, well you know not proper relationships."

"So why did you try and pretend you weren't gay? It's not like we live in the dark ages any more. No one would have cared, would they?"

"Well, my parents certainly would have."

"Yes, I can see that," I said. "Oh! Just had a thought, does this mean I don't have to go down to your mother's anymore? Please say yes, please!"

He laughed, "I suppose not."

"Yeah, win," I shouted and fist pumped the air. "It's worth all this just to get out of ever having to do that again."

"Is she that bad?" he said dejectedly.

"Oh, come on," I said. "You know she is, she makes Genghis Khan look like Graham Norton."

"Yeah, you could be right there."

"So carry on then, you were telling me why you felt you had to hide who you were."

"It just seemed the right thing to do. You see whilst I was growing up, I had never met or even come across anyone that was gay. When I started getting the feelings that I did, I just assumed it was a phase I was going through. I honestly believed everyone went through the same thing. It wasn't until I hit my teens that I realised it was much more than that and by then I had convinced myself that I didn't want to be that way."

"Can you do that?" I questioned.

"Come on Jo, you know how I was brought up, if I'd have told my parents or friends, my life wouldn't have been worth living. I just wanted an easy life, coming out would have just made things too complicated and difficult. I just wasn't prepared to risk it. I naively believed that I could just forget about it, sex wasn't an issue; I never did have a particularly high libido so I just assumed that satisfying my urges with a woman would be the same as satisfying them with a man."

"And is it?" I asked.

"No," he said. "It isn't. What I hadn't realised in my inexperience was that by denying myself who I was, I was also denying myself the chance of truly falling in love. In the choice that I made, I had unknowingly shut the door on any possibility of finding that happiness."

"Oh George, that's so sad," I said. "Go on."

This was the most I had ever known George talk, clearly there was a lot to explain and I was finding it hugely fascinating.

"I focused very much on my career," he continued. "Telling myself that I didn't need love or relationships, I became a workaholic. I had the odd fling with a woman, more to keep up appearances than anything, but none of them lasted. Then, as I got older I realised that I wanted a family. It was only when I met you that I truly thought I might just get away with it. You were so clever, so full of life and energy. I really did fall for you as a person. This is the woman I want as the mother of my children I told myself and I made sure I got you."

"I don't know whether to be flattered or insulted," I said. "I always did say you married me for my child bearing hips."

"Don't underestimate yourself, Jo. I do care for you very deeply."

He continued.

"We settled into our married life and things were OK for a while. I know I was never any great shakes in the bedroom department, but in fairness you never complained."

"Can't deny that," I said. "Guilty as charged."

"I figured as long as I could get away with the bare minimum that everything would be OK. Don't get me wrong here, I wasn't just going through the motions, I didn't hate making love to you, it just sort of never felt right. I never felt connected to you in the way that I knew I should."

"It's OK," I said. "Carry on; this is better than a Radio 4 play."

"Charming," he retorted. "So glad the story of my miserable life is proving to be so entertaining."

"Hey, hang on there, mate, it's my miserable life too don't forget."

"Sorry", he chortled. "I suppose it is. Anyway, I had my work and you and the house, so I just put it all to the back of my mind. Then, Rebecca came along and added a wonderful new dimension to things. I was so thrilled to be a dad."

"Yeah, fair enough," I said. "Can't fault you on that one."

"Thank you, that means a hell of a lot."

I couldn't believe how easy our conversation had become; we were talking, properly. Talking as the people we were and not as the people we pretended to be. It was so refreshing.

"The upshot was, that in order to keep our life together going, I had to shut down all my feelings and emotions and become the cold hard-hearted person you all saw. The only way I could deal with it, was to not deal with it at all. I was a coward and I escaped at every opportunity I could. The struggle was when I was at home; it just reminded me of what a terrible person I was.

"I knew what I had done to you and I had no idea how I could make it better. The nicer you were to me, the guiltier I would feel. It wasn't until I met Philip that I realised just how much of a fraud I was. Finding him was like the light being turned on in my life."

This comment did send a slight pang of sorrow through my heart. I had tried so hard to be the right person for him.

"So how and when did you meet him?" I said.

He pondered for a moment. "I suppose it's about two months ago now. We met at the club where he performs. I'm sure you've guessed by now that I wasn't always working when I was away. I would usually tag a day or two on to the end of a trip just to avoid coming home."

I suppose I should have been angry at this statement. But his story was so sad and the realisation of just how much life we had lost, made everything that had happened in the past seem inconsequential.

"I did kind of wonder," I said. "So was it love at first sight then?"

"No, not at all," he smiled. "I had gone to the club with a client from out of town. They had heard how good it was supposed to be and asked if I would take them. There were so many people; gay and straight just having a good time and being themselves. It was such an eye-opener, I just found the whole thing so liberating. They do seriously have the best floor show in town, drag or not, it's bloody good entertainment. I'll have to take you sometime.

"Anyway, Philip was schmoozing round the crowd before his set and he came over to talk to us. He must have seen something in me because after his act he came over and asked if he could buy us a drink. We all got chatting and we spent the rest of the evening with him.

"At the end of the night we all went back to our hotel, the client went up to bed and Philip and I stayed in the bar, just talking. I still to this day don't know why I did it, but I found myself asking him if he would like to come up to my room. I had no idea what I would do with him when I got him there, or even if I really wanted to do anything, my instincts must have taken over. I just couldn't resist him."

He stopped and looked concerned. "Are you OK with this, Jo? You can tell me to shut it, I would understand if you didn't want to hear anymore."

"No, No, I'm fine," I reassured him. "Just don't give me any gory details, OK?" I couldn't quite understand why, but I was totally mesmerised by his story,

"Err, no, I won't; well, we got up to the hotel room and Philip could obviously tell I had never done anything like this before. He was just amazing, so gentle and kind. Without wanting to hurt your feelings, I had the best sex of my life and had feelings I didn't even know I could have."

Hang on, that sounds vaguely familiar: it would seem we had both now experienced the revelation of good sex.

"So, then what happened?"

"We spent the night together and then went our separate ways. I told him there was no way I could see him again, he knew I was married and understood things were complicated so we left it there. I came back here and tried to forget about him, but I couldn't.

"Every time I went away, I would go and see him. He started to want a proper relationship and was trying to persuade me to tell the truth and admit to you what had been happening, but I just couldn't. Whatever you think of me Jo, I was not about to leave you and Rebecca, even if I had fallen in love with someone else.

"It was when you went on your girls' night out that I realised things were going to come to head and that it wouldn't necessarily be me that brought them there. We'd both reached out limits, we're just so lucky that we more or less did so at the same time."

We both sat for a moment, thinking our own thoughts, in an easy silence so different from the awkwardness earlier.

"Well," I said, stretching. "That's one hell of a morning, I'd say."

"You are OK, aren't you?" he questioned. "You're not pretending to be, so can you make a break for the kitchen to get the knives or something?"

"No, no, I'm not; I mean I am OK with it. To be honest, I just feel exhausted now, but weirdly, strangely content at the same time."

"Do you want me to leave?" he said cautiously.

"No, I don't think so," I said. "I think what you should do is go and have a shower and get changed, whilst I make us some lunch." I stood up.

"Rebecca will be back soon, let's just let things be for today shall we? We can talk some more when she's gone to bed. You are staying over I take it?"

He looked surprised.

"Well, yes, if that's OK with you?"

"Right then, go sort yourself out and I'll meet you in the kitchen in about half an hour." I started to go towards the door.

"Jo," he called.

"What?" I said, turning back.

"Thank you." He came up to me gave me a huge hug, a proper heartfelt squeeze and a kiss on the cheek. "You are amazing, you know."

"Yeah, yeah, whatever," I said and walked into the kitchen.

11
Nothing like a Dame

George and I sat and had a very jolly lunch. There was no tension; no lies or hidden agendas just relaxed conversation and a lot of catching up.

Rebecca returned when we were having coffee and was genuinely surprised to see us in the kitchen together.

"Daddy, you're back." She rushed over and gave him a big hug and plonked herself on his knee.

"Hello kitten," he said, giving her a kiss on the cheek.

"Is everything all right, why are you and Mummy sitting in here? You've been talking haven't you? You're not getting a divorce are you? I had a feeling you would, you know."

"No," I said calmly. "Nothing like that, everything is fine. Becca; your dad and I have just been sorting a few things out. I promise you have nothing to worry about."

"I would understand, you know," she said. "Two of my friends have just gone through divorces. Melanie Jacobs has a lady come into school twice a week at lunchtime to talk to her about how she's coping. It's all very organised these days you know."

George and I both laughed.

He glanced over to me, "Your Mum and I are not getting divorced. Yes, there will be some changes, but for the better, I promise."

"Phew," she said. "That's all right then, I'm not sure I could cope with the counselling thing, the woman that does it smells funny. Mum you haven't forgotten we have rehearsals this afternoon have you?"

Imelda had called an emergency meeting of the panto cast. I had completely forgotten, not surprisingly really; even I could be excused for letting that one slip.

"I had actually," I said. "But it's fine."

"OK, can I go up to my room for a bit? Josie has lent me a new CD and I want to download it onto my iPod before we go."

"Course you can," said George. He looked across to me, "Rehearsals?"

"Yes, you remember," I said. "We're doing the village panto, I did tell you."

"Ah yes, the dark and terrible world of amateur dramatics, how's it going?"

"Awful, the director has got me in the chorus, I can't sing or dance and there's only me and one other woman amongst 20 uncoordinated but totally stage struck kids. Rebecca's doing well, though."

"Why on earth did you agree to be in the chorus?" he laughed. "I know you wanted to try out some new things, but do you seriously think that's going to help?"

"It seemed like a good idea at the time. I have tried to get out of it, but the woman who runs it wouldn't let me."

George laughed. "Jo, you're a grown up for God's sake, believe it or not you don't have to do anything if you don't want to."

"I know," I said pathetically, "but she's scary and she shouts a lot and she says I'll mess up all the choreography if I quit now."

"You'll mess it up a whole lot more if you stick at it and still can't do it!" he said grinning.

"I don't know what else I can do. I hate letting people down; I did say I would help backstage, but this woman just won't let me off the hook. I'm sure she's making me do it because she knows I'll end up looking ridiculous."

"Oh, I hardly think that's true do you? Look, just go in there this afternoon and tell her you're not going to be in the chorus and that's that."

"I can't," I whimpered, "she'll get cross. Will you take Rebecca? You can tell Imelda that I've got some horrendous contagious disease and I can't be near people for at least the next three months. Please."

"No," was the firm response. "You can do this, Jo. Just march up to her and tell her."

"Oh, OK then," I said jokingly dejected, getting up from the table.

"Go on," he laughed. "I tell you what, if you do it, I'll take us all out for tea at The Crown, how about that?"

"Bloody hell, George! Are you trying to kill me off? There are only so many surprises a girl can take in a short space of time, you know, OK you're on."

I leaned over and held out my hand, he shook it with a big grin on his face.

When Rebecca and I arrived at the hall I glanced around the room to see if I could spot Imelda. She was talking to a woman I hadn't seen before and seemed to be a little upset.

Perhaps not the right moment, I told myself. But then I could hear George's voice in my head saying:

"Jo, just go and bloody do it."

I walked over as her conversation ended.

"Imelda," I said timidly, "could I have a word please?"

"Yes, Jo what is it?" came a curt response.

"Well, it's about me being in the chorus," I said. "I'm terribly sorry, but I don't believe it is fair to compromise your wonderful production by putting a less than competent dancer amongst such other talented individuals. So I'm afraid I'm not going to do it. I will happily help backstage if you want me to."

For the spur of the moment, I considered that to be a pretty good speech; her response took me aback a little though.

"Fine, whatever," she said. "I couldn't care less, I have far bigger problems than your petty insecurities to deal with, speak to Jim he's in charge backstage. If he can make use of you then that's fine." She flounced off to talk to Ian Henderson.

I stood for a moment astonished that I had got away with it and then went and found Jim. He was more than happy to welcome me as a part of his backstage crew and I was put in charge of stage right props; a very important job, I was told. Imelda called the rehearsal together and I very soon found out why her response to me had been so sharp.

"Darlings," she said in her usual over dramatic way. "Darlings, I have some terrible, terrible news for you all. Peter Long, our wonderful and long serving dame has been in a horrendous accident."

Gasps echoed round the room. Imelda continued.

"He'd come up with the idea of doing a free fall parachute jump in full costume as a way of getting some publicity for the show, but unfortunately something went wrong."

Murmurs of shock went round the room as we all pictured the local dame hurtling to her death. What an awful way to die.

"It seems that his bloomers got caught in the lines when he landed and he fell over backwards just as the wind picked up and was dragged by his chute and dropped down a ten foot ditch. The good news is the local paper got some fabulous pictures and it's going to be front page news. The bad news is he's broken his leg in three places and fractured his collar bone and he won't be able to do the show."

"Oohs" and "aahs" could be heard and much chattering commenced.

"Quiet, quiet, please," she boomed. "Unless we can find someone else by next Thursday's rehearsal, I'm afraid that for the first time in 20 years we will have to cancel our annual panto."

More oohs and aahs.

"I see little point in continuing with rehearsal today or tomorrow, so please all go home. I will let you know if we manage to find anyone."

Poor guy... Bloody brilliant timing for me though.

Rebecca and I went home to find George was sitting in the garden reading the paper.

"You're back early girls," he smiled.

I looked at him sitting in the chair, so relaxed, so different. I had got to know more about him in one day than I had in fifteen years.

"Oh yes, Daddy," chirped Rebecca giddily. "You'll never guess what's happened!"

She recounted the whole sorry tale about poor Peter and his parachute incident.

"So now," she said, "we may not be able to do the show and I won't get to go on stage and it's all so disappointing."

"There, there, kitten," he said. "I'm sure they will be able to find someone."

"I'm not so sure," I said. "Seems the reason this guy has done it for so long is because no one else will. Getting dressed up as a woman in these parts does not quite carry the level of kudos that it might elsewhere," I laughed.

"Ah, I see," said George. "And what of you Jo, in all this high drama did you tell Madame Director you weren't willing to be in her chorus line?"

"Yes, yes, I did," I said triumphantly. "I managed to get in there before all this kicked off so I'm afraid you owe me a slap up dinner."

"Well done," he said. "Good for you." He folded his paper and placed it on the table.

"Right then, out for tea it is. If you ladies would like to go and make yourselves even more beautiful I will meet you at the car in 20 minutes."

"We're going out for tea!" squealed Rebecca. "But we never go out for tea, well not altogether anyway. OMG, this is fab. Can I wear my blue dress Mum?"

"Yes, I suppose," I said resignedly.

"Brilliant!" She rushed into the house.

I leaned over and gave George a kiss on the cheek.

"Thanks George, you've made one little girl very happy."

"Long overdue Jo, don't you think?"

"I know, but we can talk about it all later, for now let's just all enjoy being a family, yeah?"

"Course."

As I walked towards the house, I saw him reach for his phone and start texting. I knew it would be to Philip.

How was this all going to play out? Yes, he'd told Rebecca that we weren't getting a divorce, but we couldn't just pretend nothing had happened, could we?

I went and got ready and then we all went out for dinner.

Rebecca was in heaven: not only was she out with both her parents, but they were even getting on together, laughing and joking. I could tell she was bemused by it all, but enjoying it far too much to try and fathom what had happened. And why should she? It wasn't her job to work all this out; it was ours.

We got home and Rebecca dutifully went up to bed.

"Coffee, George?" I asked.

"Brandy for me, I think," he replied. "Want one?"

"Oh, why not?"

We moved to the sitting room and once again took our designated places on our respective sofas.

"That was good fun," he said. "Cheers." He held his glass aloft.

"Cheers." I did the same.

"So where do we go from here, George?"

"I'm not sure I know," he said.

"Well, what does Philip have to say about it all?" I asked.

"I think he's in as much of a state about it as we are to be honest. He didn't believe for one minute that I would come clean."

"Knows you well then, obviously," I joked.

"Ha-ha, very funny."

"Well, what do you want to do? Do you want to move out and live with Philip?"

"I don't know; I don't want to leave Rebecca," he hesitated. "Or you."

"Me! How do I feature in this?"

"You feature because you have been a huge part of my life and you're Rebecca's mum. We may not be man and wife in any true recognised sense, but today has shown me that we can still be good parents and we need to be together to do that."

"I suppose," I said. "But what about you and Philip how will that work then?"

"Well, I did give it some thought whilst you were out and I think if we were all willing, it could still work as it is now. I would spend most of the week away as I always have and come home in-between. Rebecca's used to me being away so she won't notice any difference. I could come home weekends and we could do things as a family. I'd like the chance to try and make up for some of our lost time, you know, do the things we always should have done. What do you think?"

"I don't know," I said. "Will Philip be happy with that?"

"I think he will be."

"So, you don't think we should tell Rebecca the truth then?"

"What that her dad has turned out to be gay and has run off to live with a drag queen from Leeds? Hmm...Tough one. Err, no I don't think so, do you?"

"Well, I'm not sure you should put it quite like that, but maybe she does have the right to know. She's going to find out one day."

"Yes, I know, I'm just not sure that now is the right time. Christ, I'm still trying to come to terms with it."

"So, what you're saying is, you want to carry on just as we are and see how it goes?"

"Pretty much, I realise it's a big ask Jo, but I promise things will not be like they were before, hell I'll even babysit for you as much as you like if you want."

I laughed, "You can't babysit your own child, George."

"Yeah, yeah, you know what I'm saying though."

"I do." I sipped my brandy and gave the whole matter some thought.

"OK, let's see how we get on for the next few weeks," I said. "We'll review it as and when we need to. I can't promise any more than that."

"That'll do for me," he said once again raising his glass.

I looked across at this new found man, a man with a sparkle in his eyes and a relaxed open expression on his face. He looked ten years younger and somehow devilishly handsome. Was him being out of reach making him seem irresistible?

Don't go there, Jo, I told myself. Just don't go there.

We finished our brandy and headed off to our respective rooms.

I fell asleep with a calmness I had not felt for a long time. It had been a hell of a day and yet so many things had been put right. Explanations had been given, excuses made: all seemed to make sense.

The future on the other hand was a little less certain. Could we find a way to make this work? We both loved Rebecca that was true, but was it realistic to believe we could maintain the pretence of playing happy families? I could feel no reason why not; after all we'd spent years playing unhappy families and been brilliant at it.

The Sunday was wonderful. We had a proper family day. Brunch in the morning, out for a long walk in the afternoon and a rather grand Sunday lunch in the dining room to celebrate our new found family life.

It was as evening fell that I started to tune back into the real world. For a couple of days, I had managed to put to the back of my mind that tomorrow I was burying a true friend. I was absolutely dreading it.

During the course of the weekend I had almost convinced myself that it hadn't happened. I even thought about how I would go into the library on Monday for our usual chat. I would tell Vera the events of the weekend and she would give her usual sound and non-judgemental advice. But of course that wasn't going to happen.

George had been intending to head back to Leeds on the Sunday night. But on hearing that Rebecca and I were going to Vera's funeral on Monday he changed his plans and said he would come with us.

"You don't have to," I said. "It's not like you even knew her."

"I know, but it will obviously be hugely traumatic for you and Rebecca, and I think I should be there to support you both."

"Well, that's very sweet of you George. Thank you."

He gave me a hug and a kiss on the cheek.

"Now go to bed and try and get some sleep, eh?"

"Yes, yes, I will," I said. "Night, George."

I didn't sleep, of course. I was too preoccupied with the events of tomorrow and just couldn't switch off. Just get through it, I told myself one day, that's all it is. I hated funerals with a passion; they seemed to be such a dreadful way of saying goodbye to someone. All that grief and sadness, compacted into one place. It was all so intense. I had long expressed a wish that when I died, I was to be disposed of in a municipally appropriate way; but with no service, no church, no mourners. Just a bloody big party somewhere where everyone could have a good time and hopefully raise a glass or two in my name. Grief to me was something personal and private not something to be stifled and hidden in public, 'stiff upper lip' and all that.

I had never lost anyone close to me before. Both my parents were still alive somewhere as far as I knew. All the funerals I had been to in the past were for people I hardly knew, extended family members or people I had worked with. I always left them feeling traumatised. Not because I had felt particularly sorry about the person that had died, but because I couldn't bear to see their nearest and dearest so distressed. No, I wasn't going to put my friends and family through that. Cardboard box and a knees up for me.

133

12
We Danced the Light Fandango

Monday morning dawned as it inevitably would and I woke up feeling tired, I guessed I had probably only managed a few hours' sleep. I donned the obligatory black and went downstairs to find Rebecca and George had done the same. We sat and had a quiet breakfast each stealing themselves against the sadness that was to become the main part of the day.

The service was at 10.00am. At least it's early and gets it over with, would be worse if we had to wait until the afternoon. We drove to the village and parked in the pay and display car park. The chances of us getting near the church would be slim. Besides, it was a lovely sunny morning and the walk to the church was by the river. We were by no means alone on the path, quite the opposite. There were throngs of people walking down with us; it was strangely silent, apart from the odd good-natured, "Morning."

As we strolled along by the river I found myself soothed by the babbling sound of the water. This place with its hills and Dales, streams and rivers made me very aware of the eternity of nature. The notion that this landscape would remain unchanged and still be as stunningly beautiful whether we were there or not was somehow reassuring.

When we arrived, we found the church was already three quarters full. I guessed at about 300 people. We found Beryl and Jean and sat with them.

Although Vera had said no flowers, the church was heaped with them; but not the usual shop bought wreaths of meaningless chrysanthemums. It was full of wild poppies, foxgloves and meadowsweet, plus a fair smattering of cow parsley which I couldn't help thinking must have come from the back of Beryl's barn.

People had made their own tributes, from their own gardens, and hung them on the walls, at the end of pews, in the highest corners and the lowest steps. It was a beautiful sight, more befitting of a wedding than a funeral. In pride of place resting against the altar was our giant teapot.

It got to 10.00am and people were still trying to find places to sit. In the end, the vicar had to get more chairs from the vestry and squeeze people down the outer aisles.

The dreaded moment arrived and the vicar went to the back of the church to await the arrival of the coffin.

The taped music which had been some kind of choral type chant stopped and surprisingly Procol Harum's *Whiter Shade of Pale* began to play. The coffin was carried in and I was touched to see one of the bearers was Bill and another was Jean's husband. There was one young looking boy of about 20 who was apparently her great nephew, he and his family and flown in all the way from New Zealand to be there.

It was at that moment I realised just how little I knew my new friend.

She had been one of the most influential people in my life and yet I knew nothing about her. I felt very ashamed of how one sided our relationship had been and wished I could have had more time with her.

The first launch of hankies came forth as the coffin was carried the short distance down the aisle and laid to rest for the service. I held out knowing if I started this early on in proceedings I would be a total wreck by the end.

It took some doing.

"Family and friends," said the vicar.

"I welcome you here on this sad day to bid farewell to our much loved friend and relation, Vera Elizabeth Bailey. It is, I

135

think, fair to say that around these parts Vera was somewhat of a legend, a staunch pillar of the community and a force to be reckoned with." A titter of laughter went around the church.

"Ever giving of herself to anyone in need, she will be greatly missed and never replaced. Having lived in the Dale for some 40 years she has become as much a part of this village as the stone walls that surround it. No mean feat for an offcumden." Another titter.

"But how many of us knew of Vera's life before she came to our Dale? She was 44 when she moved here with her husband John. No age at all considering she was 89 when she left us. As a good friend and a true confidant, I think perhaps the time has come to let you all in on Vera's secrets. She will not mind, I can assure you. She was a modest and unassuming person with regards to her own achievements, which far outnumber prize winning jam or making the best scones in the Dale. We all know her determination for raising heaven knows how much money for charities both at home and abroad. Also, her commitment to running the local library, but these things are nothing in comparison to her life before we met her. You are all I'm afraid, in for somewhat of a shock. And I do mean shock. What follows is the true story of Vera Bailey and in parts it is quite harrowing and I apologise in advance to those of you of a sensitive nature."

He gestured to a young girl of about 19, who stood up from the choir stall and walked over to the pulpit.

"Vera left school when she was 14 determined to be a nurse. She was unquestionably bright and talented and got a place at The Royal College of Nursing. She trained during World War II and saw first-hand the devastation caused by the Blitz, often putting her life at risk to try and save others. In recognition for her selfless behaviour it was suggested she furthered her war efforts by joining Queen Alexandra's Royal Army Nursing Corps.

"By the time she was 20, she had been posted to France, Italy, and the Far East.

"When she was 21, she was part of a team of British Army Medics posted to Germany. On the 15th April 1945 Germany surrendered the concentration camp at Bergen-Belsen over to the British and Vera was part of the medical team that went in.

"The following is a brief extract from the official records of the time.

In the preceding weeks, the Germans had deposited in No.1 Camp over 60,000 prisoners; mostly Jews transported from other concentration camps threatened by the Allied advance. These tormented prisoners had lived and, in many cases, died in Belsen, in appalling conditions of starvation, dehydration and lack of shelter.

Unsurprisingly, the camp was a breeding ground for typhus, dysentery, and tuberculosis. Faced with such epidemics, the authorities gave up their efforts to deliver even the most basic requirements to sustain human life.

Reminiscent of Dante's Inferno *– The British discovered 20,000 emaciated naked corpses lying unburied on the open ground or in the barrack blocks. Some inmates had literally starved to death, where they lay, too weak even to drag their wasted bodies away from the typhus-infested corpses that surrounded them.*

The liberators also encountered around 50,000 'survivors'. With ribs protruding through taut dry skin, bellies distended, these shaven-headed 'living skeletons' lay or sat in their own filth on the open ground or in the tiered bunks of the camp's barrack blocks.

Despite the team's best efforts, 13,000 Belsen inmates died after liberation. Some inmates had been starved for so long that they had lost the ability to digest

*the rations that well-meaning British soldiers offered
them; within minutes of taking a biscuit, some inmates
just passed away.*

*Largely through trial and error, the medical staff de-
veloped special nutritious, but easily-digested
concoctions for the inmates. Undertaking these relief
efforts took a heavy psychological toll on the British
medics. One doctor commented that if they did not get
blind drunk each night they would all 'go stark staring
mad'."*

The young girl stepped down from the pulpit and went and
sat down.

"Let us all now sing hymn number 427, *For the Beauty of
the Earth*," said the vicar. "Please stand."

"Bloody hell," said Beryl. "I'd no idea our Vera had done
that. Had you?"

"No, no I didn't," I said. "How on earth would you ever be
able to deal with something like that?"

George grabbed mine and Rebecca's hands and gave them
a little squeeze.

"Hang on in there girls, you're doing great. This is heavy
stuff isn't it; I wish I'd met her now, quite some lady then?"

"Apparently," I said, still stunned. "Far more so than we'd
ever realized."

We dutifully did our best with the hymn, but most of us
were still reeling from the upset of the passage we had just
been read. I couldn't imagine how she must have felt: a young
girl faced with that level of horror and human misery. We sat
after the hymn to be further confronted with yet more tragedy
from Vera's life.

An older girl in her twenties went on to continue Vera's
life story.

"Having stayed on in Germany for a year after the war had
ended, Vera had met and married a young British army

officer. They came back to London and settled in the suburbs where Vera carried on nursing and her young army officer found a job working in the city. Unfortunately, her husband could not readjust after the war. The horrors he had witnessed would not leave him. He suffered from what we would now call post-traumatic stress disorder. This resulted in uncontrollable bouts of drinking that ended in beatings for Vera. She knew that he was suffering from mental trauma and tried to help him as much as she could. She even managed through her connections at the hospital to get him psychologically assessed, but little was known then about how to combat such symptoms and he never really got better.

"The tragedy of their lives together came to a devastating head when, after yet another bout of drinking, he came home and beat Vera. She was seven months pregnant and was beaten to the point she had to be hospitalized; she lost her baby and also the ability to have any more children. Her husband was arrested unable to recall any of what had happened.

"The following day once he had sobered up, he was told what he had done. He had no recollection of his actions and was sickened and appalled to learn that not only had he beaten his pregnant wife, but that he had also caused the death of his unborn child. Unable to deal with his guilt, he hung himself in his prison cell later that same day."

"Jesus," whispered Beryl. "It's like being in a Catherine Cookson novel. Boy, am I going to need a stiff drink after this. Poor old love, what a life, eh?"

"I know," I said. "I can't believe it."

The second girl stepped down.

"Hymn number 349, *One More Step*. Please stand," said the vicar.

We sang and sat and this time a woman in her early thirties took to the pulpit.

139

"Vera spent the next 15 years devoted to her nursing and travelled all over the world working with the Red Cross. She went to Africa, Asia and South America. If there was war, earthquake, flood or famine she would be there. She dodged bullets, suffered horrendous bouts of illness and on one occasion was even taken hostage by a band of Columbian bandits.

"She met her second husband John, a doctor, whilst working in Ethiopia. On finishing their tour of duty, they decided they had earned a sabbatical and found a small village in the Yorkshire Dales that they could escape to.

"Having never intended to stay long, they wanted time to rebalance and recover a little normal life before they headed out on yet another adventure. They never did. They had five years of blissful peace before John was diagnosed with cancer. Despite all Vera's experience and wonderful nursing expertise, he died a year later. Vera was all of 49 years old."

The vicar came forward. "Hymn number 478, *Make Me a Channel of Your Peace*. Please stand."

The melody of the song was soft and gentle and angelically sung by the local primary school children. If you were of a cynical nature you may think the vicar had deliberately engineered the whole thing, just to give you that extra kick in the guts; clever man.

I managed it to verse two before the tears came flooding. Rebecca bless her, seeing me crying also joined in, which left poor old George with two distraught snotty nosed females to contend with.

We were, however, far from alone; it seems this soft melody was the downfall for many a stiff upper lip. Having managed to hold themselves together for so long, this gathering of family and friends had gone past the point of no return.

The vicar stepped forward once again.

"My dear, dear friends, I realise that his morning's service has been more of a revelation than a farewell. Vera was one of my closest friends and I know how much the events of her life at times troubled her. I will feel eternally privileged that she chose to share with me what she felt she had no cause to share with anyone else. As far as she was concerned her troubles were her troubles, she never wanted to burden anyone else with the misery and sadness she had both witnessed and suffered.

"Before our last song, I am going to read you something that Vera wrote herself. Strange you may think that she could have prepared something for her own funeral, when she was so unexpectedly called up. However, I am sorry to say the saddest part of her story was not that she was so cruelly taken from us before her time; it was that she had recently been diagnosed with terminal cancer herself. Our best guess was that she would have had no more than about eight months to live."

Audible shock registered around the church.

Oh my God, that just makes it worse. Somewhere, some drugged up little shit is going to get away with doing a bit of community service; in exchange for robbing this wonderful, giving human being of the last few months of her life. I was furious.

The vicar continued.

"True to form, she didn't want anyone to know. She wanted people to treat her as they always had."

The vicar took out a sheet of paper and began to read.

"My wonderful family and friends, thank you so much for turning out on what I will no doubt guess is a bloody miserable rainy day.

If by any chance it's sunny, get yourselves the hell out of the church and enjoy it whilst you can. Those of you who are local will know it doesn't happen very often."

A soft laugh rippled round the church.

The vicar continued.

"I have had an extraordinary life.

I have seen things that most of you would never want to contemplate in your worst nightmares and I confess that many of them still come back to haunt mine.

I have however also seen how amazingly good and kind people can be, even in their darkest moments. It is these moments that I treasure, the uncompromising ability of the human spirit to rise above the wrong and always find the right, is the reason I did what I did for so long.

As long as people are faced with struggles and adversity, though often through no fault of their own, there should be people willing to be there to help them. I did my stint of war and death and watching people starve till I couldn't take it anymore. The place I found healing, calm and peace was here in these beautiful green hills and amongst these wonderful giving and caring people.

Be proud of what you have here. Never forget how rare and special it is. I have travelled all over the world and never found a better place to call home.

Thank you.

Thank you for taking me in when I was wounded of spirit and for rekindling my faith in human nature. We truly do live in God's own country.

Now piss off all of you and get to the pub. I want my wake to be the stuff of legend!

Love Vera. Xx"

The vicar laughed, "Please excuse the swearing: her words," he looked skyward, "not mine."

He continued, "We will end today's service with an unconventional song and we are blessed, or I think we are, that several members of the local rock band are here to aid us in saying our final farewells.

"I would ask you all to sing out your very best, even if it sounds the worst, to the memory of our treasured Vera Elizabeth Bailey. May God give her peace and the best cloud in the heavens, Amen."

A chorus of 'Amens' sounded softly round the church.

In an unexpectedly loud voice, the vicar shouted, "Ladies and Gentlemen, I give you Queen's, *We are the Champions*."

I couldn't see a single person that didn't join in. By the end of the song everyone had their arms in the air, holding hands, swaying side to side in true rock concert fashion, even George joined in.

It was a wonderful, uplifting, but hugely sad experience. Vera, I'm sure knew exactly the effect it would have. We all left the church laughing, wiping away a tear maybe, but with huge smiles on our faces.

She had asked that everyone leave the church before the coffin was carried out. Saying one goodbye, she felt, was quite enough. Several people, including myself, did go forward to say a personal goodbye. I offered my condolences to the small group of family that turned out to be her deceased brother's family from New Zealand and her second husband John's only surviving sister. They were to go on to the crematorium for a very brief family service, but would join us for the wake later.

Walking out into the bright sunshine was somehow heartening. The darkness of the church had been so fitting for the darkness of the tales that had been retold, but now it was time to smile. To acknowledge the true greatness of this unsung heroine, to listen to and tell our own stories of how this brave yet totally modest woman had affected our lives.

The walk to the pub was such a contrast from the walk to the church; everyone was chatting and noisy and full of approbation at the revelations about '*Our Vera*'.

On arrival, there was champagne poured and a beautiful buffet laid out. All apparently given free of charge by the landlord, as a gesture of his love and respect for Vera. It's fair to say that much wine was drunk and many a story told. George had said he would drive, so I took full advantage of the chance to give my friend a good send off and got to say the least, respectably rat arsed.

We stayed until about 4.00pm; Rebecca had understandably found the day somewhat challenging and was ready to go home. We left the party in full swing and from what I could tell, felt sure it could go down as legendary without any more help from me.

I got home, got changed and went and made us all a cup of tea. The sun was still shining so I took mine out into the garden, to the view of those wonderful hills that Vera had loved so much.

I raised my mug in the air and said, "Cheers, Vera, wherever you may be, give 'em hell! Goodbye my friend."

13
Moonlit Madness

The next few days passed with much reflection and sombre mood.

George had to legitimately be away on business, but at least had been honest enough to say he would be staying with Philip. I didn't mind, he would be back at the weekend and that was all that mattered.

We tried to resume our lives as normal, but Rebecca had found Vera's funeral very traumatic. Like me, she couldn't get over how much sadness Vera had encountered throughout her life.

"Mum," she said, "the next time I start complaining about not having the right trainers or the right clothes, I want you to just say one word to me: Vera."

"That's very sweet, hun," I said.

"No, I mean it. I can't believe how pathetic I can be sometimes. It made me so sad to hear all that stuff about her, but I'm so glad I did. I'm going to ask at school if there are any volunteer projects I can get involved in. I think I need to do something constructive, something that would make Vera proud."

"Oh Becca," I went and gave her a big hug. "That's a wonderful idea and just for the record, I'm already proud of you."

I wondered how many other people were sitting around having the same kind of thoughts. Would these revelations have a knock on effect? Perhaps we would become even more of a community than we already were?

For my part, I felt more disappointed in myself than anything. Yes, you can convince yourself that it's all a matter of perspective; of course your own problems seem bigger than everyone else's. But still the triteness of my insecurities paled into total insignificance when confronted with the enormity of what Vera had dealt with.

I couldn't stop thinking about her having cancer. Not once in the conversations that we'd had did she even hint that there was anything wrong.

Was she going to tell me? Would there have been some point at which she would have confided in me? I'd never know.

Thursday came around and I went along to flower club as usual. This week Helena had decided we wouldn't be making anything and that the money we would usually spend on flowers should be donated to Vera's Tibetan Freedom Fighters' Fund. We all agreed and then went to the coffee shop.

"Well, it's going to take me a good few weeks to recover from that, I can tell you," said Beryl.

"I know what you mean," said Jean. "I've known that woman for 35 years and I hadn't got a clue she'd been through all that."

"Not to mention the cancer thing," said Caroline. "God, what a waste."

"I still can't believe she's gone," I said. "I haven't been able to go into the library since it happened, my books are overdue."

"Give 'em to me, I'll take 'em back for you." Beryl gave my hand a gentle pat.

"Thanks," I said.

"Well, at least we'll know what the little wretch caused all this will get by the end of next week," said Jean.

We all looked at her.

"Well, she's up in court on Wednesday, 11.00am Leeds Magistrates. I thought I might go down and do some good old fashioned jeering."

"I'll come with you," I said.

"Me too," said Beryl.

"Bugger I can't," said Caroline. "I'm working."

"Sounds like a road trip to me," said Beryl nudging me in the ribs. "I'll drive if you like."

We all agreed.

"Has anyone heard anything more about poor old Peter Long?" asked Beryl.

"Well, all I know is he's out of hospital and doing OK, I think. His leg's in plaster and he's got a collar for his neck," said Jean.

"Silly old bugger," said Beryl. "Fancy doing that at his age, bad enough doing it in the right gear, never mind dressed as a bloody dame!"

"God, I wish I'd been there," she chortled. "Don't suppose anyone's stepped forward to take his place have they? Not that anyone could; he was bloody good at it."

"Imelda was saying on Saturday that if they didn't find anyone by tonight they would have to cancel the show. Rebecca was so disappointed," I said.

"Well, a good dame is hard to come by round 'ere. Not on your average farmer's to do list really. Besides, they just don't have the time for the rehearsals," said Beryl. "Still be a shame if it were cancelled. I might have a word with my Bill see if he'd be up for it."

Her conversation was cut short by my mobile phone ringing. I was more than a little surprised to see it was George calling. I gestured to the others that I was going outside as I answered.

"George, what is it? Is everything OK?"

"Yeah, everything is fine, sorry to bother you; I know it's unusual for me to ring you out of the blue."

"Yes, it is, has something happened?"

"No, well, nothing bad anyway. Look, I know this is an out the box thing to suggest, but I was telling Philip about your panto problem and well, he's offered to help out. Says he's played the dame loads of times and he'd like to do it."

"Bloody hell, that is out the box!" I exclaimed. "Is he sure? I mean, how will he get to rehearsals and stuff?"

"I've thought of that one," he said. "He could come back up with me on the Thursday and stay with us over the weekend. We can both head back to work on the Monday morning."

"Oh, I don't know about that, George," I said hesitantly. "I thought we weren't going to tell Rebecca yet? This is awfully full on, awfully fast."

"No, no, I don't mean we would come up as a couple. Philip can stay in the spare room, he can be just a friend as far as Rebecca, and everyone else for that matter is concerned. I thought it would be a rather nice way for us all to get to know each other."

"I suppose," I said unenthusiastically.

"Oh, come on Jo, I think it will be good fun."

"I'm not sure I'd call it fun," I said. "Interesting maybe, but fun's pushing it a bit."

"Well, have a think about it and let me know. Philip says he'll ring this director woman himself if you can text me the number."

"Right, yes, OK." I was still thinking it over. "Leave it with me for half an hour or so and I'll come back to you."

"Well, tell me as soon as you can. We'll need to get up there for tonight if he's going to do it, won't we?"

"Yes, 7.30pm."

"OK, well, ring me back when you know. Bye for now."

"Bye."

I walked back into the coffee shop and sat down.

"You all right love?" said Beryl. "You look a bit peaky, has something happened?"

"No, it's fine," I said. "It was just George."

I hadn't told anyone about the confessions of the last few days. Funny the one person I would have told was Vera, but of course I couldn't now.

"George? What's he got to say for 'imself then?" questioned Beryl.

"Just that he knows someone that's willing to do the dame for the panto. Friend of his from work has done that kind of thing before."

"My God, that's brilliant," said Caroline.

"You don't sound too happy about it, Jo?" said Jean.

"No, I am," I said. "It's just this guy, Philip he's called, he's going to have to stay with us from Thursday to Sunday. I'm just not sure I want a house guest for that length of time at the moment, that's all."

"Oh, I'm sure it'll be fine," said Beryl optimistically. "You never know he may be a right looker and up for a bit of fun, wink, wink."

"Hmm, don't think so Beryl," I said. "I'm fairly sure from what George told me that he bats for the other side."

"Oh well, never mind, perhaps he's a good cook then," smiled Jean.

We all laughed.

"George wants me to have a think about it and let him know. What do you think I should do?"

"Well, look on the bright side, if he's a friend of George's perhaps they'll be down the pub every night. That'll keep him out of your hair and give you a bit of peace," said Beryl.

"I suppose so," I said.

149

Inexplicably, the idea of Philip muscling in on my new found friendship with George gave me unexpected pangs of jealousy.

"Tell you what, you wouldn't half score a ton of brownie points with Imelda. Bloody hell, you'd been deemed the saviour of the panto!" laughed Jean.

I tried to think what Vera would have said, but it was just so hard to judge what her thoughts would have been. My perception of her had completely changed. I no longer saw her as 'the wise old woman of the Dale', I saw her as a totally different person. I was finding it hard to reconcile the friend I had with the person she seemingly was.

"Oh well, in that case," I said, "I don't really have a choice do I? The show, as they say, must go on. I'd better text him and let him know."

I sent Imelda's number and a message saying, *OK, let's give it a go then.*

"Are you and George getting on a bit better now, Jo?" Caroline asked.

"Yes, I wondered about that," said Jean. "Someone said they'd seen you all out down the Crown the other night. He finally come to his senses has he?"

"Something like that," I said.

"And what about his little bit on the side," said Beryl. "Come clean about that as well did he?"

Oh God, they're not going to let me get away with this one.

"Kind of, it was all a misunderstanding really."

"Oh Jo, you've not let him off the hook have you? Slapped wrist and everything OK again till the next time, I thought you had more about you than that." Beryl sounded disappointed in me.

"No, honestly, it's nothing like that, I promise, I'll fill you in on it all, just not now OK, not when the funeral and the hearing and everything are all still on my mind. Please just leave it!" I was starting to get teary.

"Sorry Jo," Caroline put her arm around me. "I didn't mean to upset you."

"It's OK, Caroline. You haven't. I'm good, honestly."

"Yeah, sorry Jo," said Jean.

"Me too," said Beryl. "You know me, pushy to the point of tactless. I keep forgetting how close you and Vera were. She'd taken a real shine to you, you know Jo. Not many people got that close to her. Surprised, she never told you any of that stuff."

"Well, she didn't, did she? She was too busy sorting out my stupid insignificant problems."

My emotions were getting the better of me.

"I was so wrapped up in me I never even gave a thought to whether there might be anything wrong with her. It never occurred to me that she might need someone to talk to about her problems. And do you know what's even worse than that? Do you know what makes this whole thing so unbearable? Well, I'll tell you, I could have stopped her dying. I could have given her those extra few months that would have given her the time she should have had."

"Now come on Jo," said Jean softly. "Calm down love, you're talking daft."

"No, no, I'm not Jean you don't understand, none of you do. It is my fault, don't you see? The day she went to Leeds, she'd asked me to go with her. The one time she had asked for anything from me and I said no. I let her down. I wasn't there for her and why wasn't I? Because yet again, I'd got myself into another load of trouble that I had to sort out. Oh yes, that's right, I let my friend die because I had to go off and meet Bi..." I stopped myself. My God, I had nearly blurted it out. I'd nearly told Beryl about my meeting up with Bill!

151

"Meeting up with who?" said Beryl anxiously. "Who were you meeting up with?"

"Oh, it doesn't matter now," I said in tears.

"The point is I killed Vera; it was my fault she went to Leeds that day on her own. If I'd gone with her then that girl would never have tried anything on and she would still be alive. Don't you see I'm the reason she's dead?" I sat and sobbed and sobbed and sobbed.

"That's ridiculous," said Jean. "You can't blame yourself Jo. You didn't make that girl do what she did. No, I'm sorry I'm not having that. She's the one to blame, not you."

"She is Jo," said Caroline sympathetically. "It wasn't your fault."

"It is," I said. "I should have been there and I wasn't. The one time, the one and only time she'd asked and I'd said no." I sobbed again.

"Well, no one can change it now," said Beryl. "What's done is done. You going off on a big guilt trip isn't going to help anyone is it? Do you think Vera would want you doing that, eh? Course she wouldn't. Now come on dry your tears and stop being so bloody daft." She handed me a napkin.

"She's right Jo," said Caroline. "We could all say what if, but it doesn't change anything. What happened that day was no one's fault. Vera should have been able to go to town without needing to be protected. No one could have known what that girl was going to do, or how poor Vera would have reacted. You can't blame yourself."

I knew she was trying to be kind, but I had got myself so worked up I couldn't cope with any of them anymore.

"I'm going," I said irritated. "'I've got to get the sodding spare room ready for George's 'friend' arriving." I made quotation marks in the air without even thinking about it. I realised my mistake by Jean's expression. She had twigged something, but realised now was not the time to make comment. I paid my bill and left them to it.

As I drove home, my thoughts were full of hate and anger and guilt. The one conclusion I had come to was that whatever justice the system was willing to dole out, it would never be enough to make up for the pain this girl had caused.

I got home and decided a cigarette and a coffee were most definitely called for. After all, it's not every day you blurt out to your friends that you've killed someone and then have to come home and prepare yourself to meet your husband's lover. Whatever I had wished for in my visions of changing my life, this sure as hell wasn't it.

By the time Rebecca had got home from school, I had calmed myself enough to get over one trauma in preparation for dealing with another. I told her about Philip taking over as dame and she was over the moon.

George had texted me to say they would get home about 6.00pm, which meant we would just have time for something to eat before we headed out to rehearsal.

I'm not sure anything can ever prepare you to meet your partner's lover. The variety of my emotions as I waited for them to arrive was quite unnerving. I found myself in the mindset of wanting him to like me, similar to when you meet your boyfriend's parents but at the same time feeling jealous. I also wanted to like him; I wanted George to be happy and being in the position of disapproving would make things very difficult for us all. There was also a very large part of me that wanted George to stay as he was and just realise that he wasn't in fact gay at all and that he did love me after all. That was the one least likely to happen, I thought.

They finally arrived and I went to greet them. Philip was stunning, very fresh faced with gorgeous blue eyes. I could see immediately why he was so successful as a drag queen. The definitive pretty boy: perfect skin, perfect hair and looks that put him a good 15 years younger than his age.

Bastard. He held out his hand. I could feel it tremble as I shook it, then he leaned in and gave me a soft kiss on both cheeks.

"Hello, Jo," he said in a gentle effeminate voice. "It's so lovely to meet you."

Rebecca came bounding in.

"This is Rebecca," I said.

He greeted her in exactly the same way.

"Gosh," she said. "It's brilliant that you're here, thank you so much for saving our panto."

"It's my pleasure," he said smiling.

"Come on in, Philip," said George and led him to the sitting room. We followed them through.

"I'll just take the bags up to our rooms."

"OK, Philip please sit down, can I get you a drink or anything?"

"Oh yes, thank you, A glass of wine would be great about now."

"Yes, I bet it would," I said. "I think I'll have one too. Rebecca, you stay and chat to Philip."

I went back into the kitchen to get the wine and took a deep breath; so far so good. Rebecca would keep him entertained for a few minutes. I poured the wine and downed my first glass in one go, then refilled it and took them through.

"There you go. Cheers!"

"Cheers!" he said. "Thank you."

"Well, dinner won't be long, nothing special just lasagne, I hope that's OK?"

"Yes, that's fine, I love lasagne."

"Makes the best lasagne in the county, our Jo," said George coming back into the room.

"Do I, George? You've never said that to me before."

"Well, I'm saying it now." He swept passed me and gave me a kiss on the cheek before sitting tactfully on the opposite sofa to Philip.

"So, Philip spoke to the lovely Imelda this afternoon," he said.

"Did you, how did you get on?"

"Fine, I think she was a bit unsure at first, but once I'd reeled off all the different shows I'd done she seemed quite enthusiastic. She's very appreciative of my stepping in."

"Oh, we all are, aren't we Mummy?" chirped Rebecca.

"Yes, we are," I said, trying to sound grateful. "It really is very good of you." I stood up. "If you'll excuse me, I'll just go sort out dinner."

I left them all chatting away and I could hear Rebecca and George laughing, a clear indication that all was going well. I downed another glass of wine. God, what a day, what a week, what a year in fact. By the time I had called them in for dinner, I was starting to get a little tipsy.

"George," I said over dinner. "I'm afraid I may have had one too many to drive tonight, do you think you could take Rebecca and Philip to rehearsals? I don't need to be there now I'm just doing props."

"Course I can," he said. "I'd quite like to see Philip's début as the dame." He looked across at him and winked.

Oh please, I think I'm going to be sick.

I was jealous, I was truly jealous. I hadn't considered for one minute that I would be, but I was. Not only was this guy, charming and witty and talented, in drag he was probably better looking than me as well.

"You OK, Jo?" George asked.

"Yes, I'm fine, I think I'm getting one of my migraines that's all. I might just have an early night when you all go."

He patted my hand. "That's a good idea; you have rather been through it just lately, haven't you?"

We finished dinner and they all went out to rehearsal. I sat and drank the remainder of the bottle of wine and mulled over the events of the last few weeks. What a mess.

The wine had made me melancholy.

I was thinking of Vera and trying to reconcile my feelings of guilt and concluded that I couldn't. I then turned to George and attempted to try and understand why I should feel so jealous when less than a week ago I could barely stand the sight of him.

It's not bloody fair, I said to myself. Here I am, on my own, no one to love me, no one to make me feel wanted or special. Life is such a pile of shit.

Then Bill popped into my head; lovely, kind, gentle, unavailable Bill. If I could have just one more hour in those expert hands, the rest of my troubles would be forgotten. But I couldn't. I sat getting more and more angry and frustrated. I felt like a caged animal, as though I had no control over anything that was happening to me.

I wanted to be reckless and impulsive. I needed to do something unexpected, daring and unpredictable. My sense of needing excitement overtook me and before I had even given myself chance to think, I had got my mobile phone and sent Bill a text.

I can't stop thinking about you. I want you, and I want you now. I typed frenziedly.

A shock wave of butterflies hit my stomach like a tsunami. Good butterflies, butterflies of anticipation and the unknown. Not the butterflies of dread and anxiety and fear that I had dealt with over the last few days. I knew it was wrong and disloyal, but I didn't care, I just wanted to feel better. I knew it was betraying Beryl; but it was her that had originally suggested that Bill was something to be borrowed.

"I'll think of him as a big warm jumper," I told myself. "I can borrow him when I'm feeling cold and alone and then give him back when I feel all warm and cosy again. Where is the harm in that?"

Anyway, chances were he would send a reply saying, "sod off."

My problem then would be what to do the next time I saw him. I resolved that I would just have to make sure I never did.

I was just starting to think what a stupid cow I had been and how selfish I was for putting Bill in such an awkward position, when the text alert on my phone went.

I literally squealed with surprise. I hardly dare read it.

I can't stop thinking about you either, it said. *Can you get away?*

Yes, I can, I texted. *Where and when*? My hands were shaking.

Meet me at our old barn on the top field on moor road in ten mins.

OK.

Oh my God, this was it, this was my chance to be completely and utterly not me.

I quickly got myself ready and set off. I knew the barn he meant; it was five minutes from the house on foot.

I arrived at the field and began the short walk. The moon was almost full and cast an eerie blue light across the landscape, a soft breeze brushed against my skin and as I walked I became sensually awakened in a way I had never been before. Ahead of me lay what could possibly be the most erotic experience of my life. I was so breathless with anticipation, I felt light-headed.

I reached the barn. Bill had hung a lantern in the doorway; it cast such a warm yellow light in contrast to the cold blue of the moon.

I peeked my head around the door and saw another lantern set in a corner directing a soft light up into the hayloft. I wandered over to the ladder and climbed up.

The sight that met me was wonderful. Laid naked and resplendent on the hay was Bill, a clichéd piece of straw clenched between a cheeky smile. He looked so gorgeous and sexy, all muscle and testosterone. I knew he was there for one reason and one reason only…me. It felt as though I had been taken out of time and plonked between the pages of a D.H Lawrence novel.

"Bloody hell, you don't waste any time do you?" I laughed.

He smiled. "Shut up and get over here."

I walked over and lay down beside him. He leant on his arm and gave me a beautiful, long sensual kiss. Heaven, absolute heaven.

"Before we do anything Bill, I just want you to know, I don't want to talk about anything tonight. I just want to be with you, I want you to make me forget everything apart from being here. Is that OK?"

"Hell yes," he said. "That works for me." And with no further words, we once again shared the delights we had shared before; only this time our glorious foreplay ended with mind-blowing, passionate, full-on lovemaking. God, this guy was brilliant.

We lay silently in each other's arms for a while, gently stroking and caressing each other, completely content in our sexual fulfilment. I came to the conclusion that if George was happy being parent and partner, why not have Bill just for sex? It would make life a whole lot simpler.

I kissed him. "Thanks Bill, that was amazing."

"You're welcome," he said. "You OK?" He gently stroked my hair.

"Hell of a lot better for that," I smiled. "Are you OK?"

"Yeah, fine, must admit though I was surprised to get your text."

"Hmm, yes, sorry about that, but you are glad I did, aren't you?" I lightly teased my fingers over his chest.

"Yes, I am," he said softly. "Very glad." He kissed me again.

I pulled away. "Well, as much as I would love to stay, I have to get going." I started to get dressed.

He came up behind me still naked and wrapped his arms around my waist. "This gonna be a regular thing then is it?"

"Would you like it to be?" I said, stroking the inside of his bare thigh.

"I could be persuaded." He kissed the back of my neck.

"No strings though, right?" I said. "No complications, just sex."

"Just sex."

I turned to face him. "I mean it Bill, no 'I love you's' or commitment, both our lives are complicated enough. Just once in a while we meet up, forget the world for a couple of hours and indulge each other in totally abandoned, wanton sexual gratification. Deal?"

"Yeah, I could go for that." He smiled.

"Right then, I'm off, I'll be in touch soon." I kissed him again and left him in the lantern light of the barn.

I got home had a shower and went to bed. I didn't even hear the others get home. I slept like a log.

14
Beryl's Antics

The next few days were spent in a confusion of jealousy and guilt.

When Bill and I had met at the barn, I had been so carried away in the moment it never occurred to me to question his motives. When we met up after the fateful Friday night he had been totally adamant that nothing like that could ever happen again, so what had changed? I might have hoped his change of heart was down to my astounding prowess as a lover, but I was pretty sure there was more to it than that. Something must have happened between him and Beryl.

My pang of conscience was short lived and easily appeased by remembering Beryl and her swinging antics. If we were ever 'found out' she of all people would surely understand the difference between sex and love. Although I could question whether having sex with lots of different people is better or worse in terms of perceived infidelity, than having lots of sex with the same person.

Did that mean we were having an affair?

I thought not. Affairs had to involve spending vertical as well as horizontal time together, doing lovey-dovey things like talking and going out for dinner. I wasn't going to socialise my relationship with Bill, why would I? Time spent talking would lessen the time spent in pursuit of my new found hobby!

No, this was far simpler than an affair; this was uncomplicated, unemotional, pure physical gratification. A 'shag buddy' I learned was the correct term, definitely not an affair.

Scruples duly placated, I now just had to deal with the unexpected pangs of jealousy I was having towards Philip and George.

On the whole it was a lovely weekend, George and Rebecca had never spent this much time together with and it was so refreshing to see him relaxed and happy.

There was though, still a part of me that couldn't quite forgive him. I had loved him so much and tried so hard to make him happy. And yet here was Philip, a man it would be impossible to dislike no matter how hard I tried; who had done more to fulfil my husband in a few months than I had managed in 15 years.

I was fine when we were all together; it was like having a family friend to stay. Philip was good company, witty, educated and charmingly sensitive. I could see why George had fallen for him, but it was still a bizarre situation.

On the Friday, we had all gone out together for dinner. And on the Saturday, we went walking in the hills with a stop off at a rather cosy pub along the way for lunch. When we got home Philip insisted that he cook dinner ably assisted to my surprise, by George.

It was their stolen moments I became aware of. The knowing glance, the almost imperceptible touches, but the kiss: the kiss was the final straw.

Rebecca had gone to bed and we were all clearing up, I was bringing dishes through to the kitchen from the dining room and they obviously hadn't heard me coming. I walked in on them leant against the Aga in a full on open-mouthed kiss. It was so passionate and sensual; I stood for a moment transfixed, watching the man I had been married to all these years being so unreservedly tender and loving.

Why couldn't George have kissed me like that? I didn't know whether to feel sick, jealous or aroused. They quickly separated when they realised I was standing there.

"Sorry Jo," said George, quickly trying to recover himself.

"Yes, sorry Jo, totally inappropriate, I apologise," said Philip looking very embarrassed.

"It's OK," I said coldly. "Please just be careful that you don't get the urge when Rebecca is about; I don't want her knowing anything about this just yet."

"No, no of course not, we wouldn't. I promise," reassured George.

"Good, please make sure you don't." I put the dishes on the side and headed for the door. "Well, I'm guessing from that little display that you two would appreciate some time to yourselves. So I'll head up to bed." My tone was curt.

"No, don't feel you have to do that," said George ruefully. "We were just going to make some coffee. Please stay."

"Yes, please Jo, I'd hate you to feel you were in the way."

To give him his due, Philip said this with some degree of convincing sincerity. But I decided it would be far better to keep the moral high ground. Although taking into account my own recent indiscretions it may be my last chance to do so.

"No, I'd rather go to bed. Just try not to make too much noise." I left the room and closed the door behind me. I went up to bed feeling very lonely.

I got up late the following morning and wandered into the kitchen to be confronted with George resplendent in a pinny, frying pan on the go.

"Ah, morning Jo, sleep well? Coffee's made, there on the table. Thought we could all have a good old-fashioned Sunday brunch. If that's OK?"

"Am I hallucinating, George? Seriously, have you made real coffee using the machine? And frying pans, you actually looked in a cupboard and found things all by yourself." I sat down. "I mean, I wouldn't be surprised if I was seeing things, it has been a rather strange few weeks." I was genuinely taken aback.

"Now, come on Jo, here, let me get you a coffee." He got me a cup and poured the coffee for me.

"There, first cup of the day, always your favourite and no I don't blame you for being a bit edgy. You have had a hell of a lot to deal with." He softly patted my shoulder.

Ha, a lot to deal with. My God, if he only knew the rest!

He went back to his frying.

"No, the breakfast," he continued, "is well, well, it's sort of an apology for last night. You've been so amazing about Philip and me and you catching us last night, I know that must have been hard for you. I am deeply sorry."

"It's fine," I said unenthusiastically. "To be honest, I'm getting to the stage where nothing surprises me anymore, well apart from the sight of you in an apron cooking of course. That, I will never get over."

I took another sip of my coffee and stood up, cup in hand. "Where are Rebecca and Philip anyway?"

"They've just nipped to the village shop to get essential supplies, can't have a fry up without sausages."

"Oh right, well, I'm just going to finish my coffee outside if you don't mind. The fresh air might wake me up a bit."

He looked across at me disapprovingly. "We both know, there will be nothing fresh about that particular air, now don't we?"

"Oh, sod off George, I'm not in the mood for a lecture. Please allow me one single bloody thing that's in my control, OK!"

He walked over and put his arms around me.

"I was joking, Jo. You go and enjoy your secret cig."

I left him in the kitchen and went to my sacred spot behind the greenhouse. It was cold, damp and depressing, which pretty much summed up how I was feeling. I wandered back into the house and poured myself another coffee. Rebecca and

Philip duly returned from the shop and George produced a quite marvellous brunch for us all.

The bastard. All this time he's let me do all the cooking when clearly he could have done some if he'd wanted to. I don't see why coming out should have to include showing off a whole new set of domestic skills as well as his French kissing technique! It was all starting to get on my nerves.

We got through the meal, but conversation between the adults was uneasy. Philip was clearly feeling awkward about the night before and we were all grateful for Rebecca's oblivious chatter.

Thankfully, George suggested a trip into town for Rebecca and Philip before they headed to rehearsals, which spared us all any further need to play happy families.

I waved my cheery goodbyes from the door and closed it with a huge sigh of relief. Peace at last!

I cleared the kitchen and poured the last cup of coffee from the pot and set about catching up on emails.

Considering I was a relative newcomer to the activity I seemed to get an awful lot of them. Admittedly, mostly from people I had never heard of wanting to let me into the secret of how to make a million pounds by simply replying to their email. So kind.

But I wasn't stupid, well just the once. After that I mastered the art of spam filtering, which I was quite proud of. Not bad at all considering that if someone had asked me what it was a few weeks ago, I most likely would have suggested some kind of recipe using processed ham.

So into the junk mail went most of my inbox, leaving a note from Helena about flower club. This week we were doing architectural minimalism, using the humble spatula. On the cooking sherry again there Helena, I thought.

One from Jim, the backstage manager for the panto asking if everyone involved behind the scenes could have a meeting on the 18th. The meeting was to be held at The Crown. Could end badly, I thought, but could be fun.

The last one was from the dentist reminding me that Rebecca had an appointment on Wednesday at 9.30am, which I had of course completely forgotten.

Bugger, I thought, it's the day of Vera's court case.

It would be too late to get it changed, well not without having to wait about six months for another appointment and it was her first assessment for braces so it was pretty important.

I decided I would just have time to take her and make it to Leeds for 11.00am. It would mean getting there under my own steam rather than going with Beryl, but that might not be such a bad thing. I wasn't sure my guilt free look was sufficiently practised to be convincing in a face-to-face encounter.

Bravado is all very well when you're talking to yourself, but it's a whole different ball game in reality. I would however have to ring her to tell her.

I took the plunge there and then, and dialled her number. I was a little startled when Bill answered the phone.

"Oh, hi Bill," I said, trying to sound nonchalant. "I was looking for Beryl. Is she about? It's Jo."

Stupid cow, why did I say that? He knows it's you. For one thing, they have caller ID and for another he's heard your moans and screams in the heat of passion. God, I hated myself sometimes.

"Hi Jo, no, she's not I'm afraid. She went over to Manchester yesterday. I think she's back tonight." He sounded low.

"Really?" I said. "She never mentioned it."

"No, it was a spur of the moment thing. Can I give her a message?"

"Well, yes," I said hesitantly. "Can you just tell her that I can't drive over to Leeds with them on Wednesday? Becca's got an appointment first thing that we can't miss, so I will have to head over after."

"OK, will do." His voice was flat and tired.

"You OK, Bill? You don't sound too good."

"Yeah, yeah, I'm fine."

"You sure, has something happened? It's not Thursday night is it? God, I'm sorry, I knew I should never have sent that text. I tell you wine has a hell of a lot to answer for. I swear I'm going teetotal."

He laughed a half-hearted laugh, "No, it's not that, I promise, it's, well it's…" He stopped.

"It's what?" I urged. "Come on Bill, tell me, is it anything I can help with?"

"No love it's not. I can't, I can't talk about it."

"Bloody hell Bill, come on, talk to me, what on earth has happened? Please, you know you can trust me. Come on, you know what they say, a problem shared is next week's gossip for the village." I was trying to cheer him up.

He laughed again, "No, honestly, I'm just a bit down today. I'll be fine."

"Bugger that," I said resolutely. "Look, I'm on my own here. The others are all out at rehearsals and won't be back for ages. Why don't you come over for a coffee? You don't have to tell me anything if you don't want to, just coffee and a chat. What do you say?"

"I don't know Jo…" He was hesitant.

"Oh, go on. I'm bored off my chump here. My most exciting prospect is a pile of ironing. Please, I would love the company and I brownie promise I won't jump on you."

Another small laugh, "Well I'm definitely not coming over then."

"So I'll put the kettle on shall I?"

"OK, you win. I'll be over in about ten minutes. Bye."

"Bye."

I put the phone down feeling genuine concern for Bill. Despite my trying to convince myself that he was just my sex toy, it would appear that some semblance of the kind and caring Marjorie Primm remained.

He arrived and we went into the kitchen. He looked tired and if I am absolutely honest, as though he had been crying. I wondered whether he was telling the truth about Thursday.

"I have to say, you look like hell Bill. How do you take your coffee?" I put a reassuring hand on his shoulder.

"Thanks very much," he smiled. "I thought you were supposed to be cheering me up? White, two sugars, please."

"Sorry, but who other than a good friend can tell you the truth?"

I made the coffee and we both sat at the kitchen table.

"So, are you going to tell me what's happened?" I said.

"I'm not sure I should."

"But it definitely doesn't have anything to do with the other night?"

"No, I promise," he took my hand. "For the record, Thursday night was just as good for me, as you say it was for you."

"Well, that's a relief. Is it Beryl then? Does she suspect something?"

"No, not at all; Beryl," he hesitated, "Beryl hasn't quite been herself lately, well not since Vera's funeral anyway."

"Well, it was a great shock to all of us, we all thought we knew Vera and it turned out that we didn't. I don't think it's surprising that we're all having to do some soul searching, I know I have.

"I'm pretty sure that's the reason I texted you that night, some kind of rebellion against the grief. We all have our different ways of dealing with this kind of thing.

"So, is Beryl depressed, do you want me to talk to her?"

167

"I don't think it will help. She's not depressed exactly; more just can't give a damn any more. She's gone back to swinging." He paused. "I told you we'd got it down to every month or so?"

I nodded.

"Well, now it's at least once a week sometimes more. That's where she's gone. Some hotel in Manchester does whole weekends of it. She seems to have lost her self-control. I'm so worried about her."

"Oh, Bill," I said. "I am so, so sorry. Have you talked to her about it?"

"I've tried, but she just tells me to leave her alone. Says I knew who she was when I married her and that if I didn't like it, she'd leave."

No wonder he answered my text so readily the other night, poor man is going through the same kind of shit that I am. Ports in a storm I decided - that's what we were to each other.

"Worst of it is, she's drinking heavily and I think she's been taking some kind of antidepressants as well. I didn't even know she was on them."

Well, it would explain why she was always so bloody cheerful. There is something decidedly untrustworthy about a person who is sodding chirpy all the time.

Bill continued.

"I found an empty tablet box in the bin. I did ask the doc about it and he shouldn't have told me, but I think he knew how worried I was about her. Anyway, seems she's been on them for about two years. Two bloody years and she never even told me." He broke into a soft sob.

"Oh Bill…" I squeezed his hand and held it.

"I tried so hard Jo, I gave her everything I could. I don't see how I could have done any more. Am I that bad a husband? Am I so boring and predictable that she can only be happy pumping herself with drugs and sleeping with strangers?"

My heart filled with his pain. However much of a friend Beryl had been I was finding it hard at this moment to remember that.

"No Bill, you're not." I got up from my chair and went over to him.

"Look at me." He turned and I took his tear stained face in my hands.

"You are a wonderful, gentle man and Beryl is a fool not to see how special you are. If I had a man like you I'd thank God every day." I gave him a gentle kiss on the cheek.

"Thanks, that's kind of you." He took out his handkerchief and wiped his eyes. "Look at me, silly old soft bugger. What do I do though, Jo?"

"I'm sure it's just a phase Bill, some kind of reaction to what happened to Vera. She'll come back to you, I'm sure she will."

"Thing is though, I'm not sure I want her to. Even if she does pack in the swinging, she's still on the pills and that has to be for a reason. I think I just have to face up to it, I don't make her happy.

"I probably never have. I know she loved me once, maybe when the boys were young and we had a reason to stick together. But now, now they're off doing their own thing, we've lost our glue and I think she realises she just isn't meant to be with one person. I think I'm going to have to let her go."

My God, he really does love her. He's so unselfish he's going to let her leave rather than make her stay and be unhappy.

"Anyway." He blew his nose and sat up straight. "Enough of my sorry troubles, what about you and George? That all seems to be going better from what I hear."

If only he knew, I thought.

"Well, it is and it isn't," I said. "We are getting on better, but how can I put it..."

169

Sod it; just tell him, he's confided in me about his less than normal relationship. Why shouldn't I trust him with the exposé of mine? So I did. I told him the whole story about George and the suspected affair, then about him coming clean and telling me the truth.

He was genuinely shocked.

"Fuck me," he whispered.

"Hmm, not sure you're his type," I laughed. "No offence but you're probably a bit rugged for him, but I on the other hand, would happily do so."

"No, I mean, well, I am lost for words." And he was.

I let it sink in for a moment and drank my coffee.

"Eh Jo, and you were going through all that, with Vera dying and everything. God you're some woman. Nobody would have ever known you had all that on your plate."

"Well, it's not the kind of thing you go round telling everyone is it?"

"No, I suppose not. We are two of a kind aren't we?"

"Yep, I guess we are."

"Does explain why you decided to get in touch though. I had wondered about that.

"Funny really, do you realise that it's the only time I've been truly unfaithful to her. I mean I have slept with other women, but she's always known about it. Even decided who they would be.

"At one time she used to insist on watching, that's when I couldn't do it any more it all got a bit too strange.

"But Thursday, Thursday was different; I've never done anything like that before. Don't know what came over me, I think I just thought sod it, why not?"

"Charming," I laughed.

"Sorry, I didn't mean it like that. I meant, well, it couldn't have been just anyone, it would only have been you, although I'm not quite sure why."

"It's OK Bill, I'm teasing you. Let's not over analyse it, eh? We've both agreed it is what it is. An escape from all our other troubles and challenges. I trust you and you trust me. It's simple really."

"I suppose so," he said.

"Friends with benefits. What a wonderful way to be."

He laughed.

"I'm guessing I don't have to worry about George coming after me with a shotgun then? That's a relief."

I laughed.

"No, I don't suppose you do, not so sure about Beryl though..."

We both laughed, then looked at each other a little troubled.

15
Stupid Deaths!

Bill left promising to keep me posted on the Beryl situation and I waited for the others to come home. They bustled into the house all noise and enthusiasm, recounting stories of who had done what at rehearsals. Philip of course, was a resounding success, adored by all especially Imelda.

"He's a star," said George. "An absolute star. I don't know who the guy that did it before was, but my God, he's going to have one hell of an act to follow."

"Oh, George stop it," protested Philip. "It's only a village panto, but thanks for the kind words." He glanced, that bloody glance at him again.

"It's true, Mummy. Philip is wonderful, he can sing and dance and he's ever so funny, the show is just going to be amazing."

"That's wonderful darling," I said.

"Congratulations Philip, it sounds like you have just about everybody eating from the palm of your hand." I didn't mean to sound bitchy but I just couldn't help it. Early days, I told myself, don't be too hard on yourself.

George I think could sense that my patience had reached its limit. He suggested that he and Philip head back to Leeds that night rather than going in the morning. I was annoyed with myself for not getting a better grip of my feelings, but couldn't help being genuinely pleased when they both finally left.

I had my house and my little girl all to myself and I was damn well going to make the most of it. Yes, it was a school night but for once the rules could be bent.

We sat snuggled on the sofa, popcorn and fizzy drinks at the ready. The temptation to dig out *Priscilla Queen of the Desert* for me was almost too much; but we settled for a teen, high school type romp that was more suited to Rebecca. I didn't mind, it was just the antidote I needed to a weekend of gay husbands, drag queens and lovers.

We plodded our way through the week, in a peaceful and calm routine. No dramas or crises: just Rebecca heading out to school, having dinner together, the usual day to day stuff that a few weeks ago I never thought I could have missed.

The events of the last few weeks had been exhausting and it was nice just to 'be' for a few days. I knew it would be short lived; Wednesday would put paid to that.

I had heard nothing from Bill and took it as a sign that no news was good news.

Wednesday morning arrived and I took Becca for her appointment. We were out by 10.00am, which just gave me enough time traffic permitting, to get to the court by 11.00am.

The traffic wasn't permitting and by 10.45, I was still half an hour away.

"Bloody, sodding traffic," I cursed. "Why aren't all these bloody people at work already? How can so many people not be where they are supposed to be by this time in a morning?"

I tried to ring Jean on her mobile but couldn't get an answer. I assumed she must already be seated in the court-room and that phones had to be switched off. I left her a message so she at least knew I had tried to get there.

By 11.30 I was still nowhere near. "Pointless, fucking pointless," I yelled as I hit the steering wheel with my fists. "I might as well just turn round and go home."

So I did.

When I got back, there was a message on the answer phone from Jean. She said she would be in the coffee shop at 2.00pm if I wanted to meet her so she would fill me in on what had happened.

Caroline, bless her, had arranged to take her lunch break at the same time, so she too could be included in the debrief. Jean arrived and we all got our drinks.

"I'm so sorry, Jean," I said. "The traffic was a complete fucking nightmare; I just couldn't get into town in time. So, what happened?"

"It was a complete farce," she said. "For one thing, the previous case finished early so they bumped it up by half an hour. You would have missed it even if you had got there on time."

"Can they do that?" I said.

"I think they can do pretty much what they want to, particularly in the magistrate's court and to be honest, it was classed as a minor offence."

"Bloody cheek," I said. "It was hardly minor to poor old Vera."

"Really doesn't seem fair," said Caroline.

"So did you miss it as well then Jean?" I asked.

"No, we got there a bit too early. Just as well, otherwise none of us would have made it."

"What happened then?" asked Caroline.

"Well, it was pretty much as we'd thought. Some bleeding heart social worker pleaded a case for her. How she was driven to steal to feed her drink and drug habit. Usual stuff.

"She was given six months probation and told she had to attend a substance abuse centre once a week for a year. Like that's going to do any good!

"Beryl was furious. She started screaming and shouting at the top of her voice. One of the clerks had to take her out the room. I've never seen her so angry. But then she's not been quite herself lately. It was all just awful."

Jean stopped to take a drink of her coffee.

"Where's Beryl now?" I asked. "I thought she might be here, God she wasn't arrested was she?"

"No," said Jean. "Nothing like that, she said she needed some time on her own to calm down. I asked her if she wanted me to stay with her and she said no. So I caught the train back. Last I saw of her, she was heading into a pub just across the road from the court."

"So that's it then," I said. "The system deems justice to have been done. What a load of crap."

"'Fraid so," said Jean. "Think all we can do now, is try and put it behind us and remember Vera for the person she was without all this horrible stuff dragging her memory down."

"I suppose so," said Caroline.

"It still stinks," I said. "But no, you're right Jean. We can't let this girl tarnish her memory. We need to do something positive now, something that will clear the air."

We all sat silent for a few minutes.

"I know," I blurted. "What about a charity fund raiser? We could start a Vera Bailey trust and have a ball or something. She would love that. We could make it an annual event. What do you think?"

"Oh yes," said Caroline. "I think that's a wonderful idea."

"Yes, yes, I agree," said Jean.

"Great," I said. "I'll give it a bit more thought and let you know what I come up with, assuming you're OK for me to sort it?"

"Fine by me," said Jean.

"I can't think of anyone better," said Caroline.

"Great, ladies: here's to putting this sorry mess behind us and giving the name of Vera Bailey some oomph for the future. Cheers." I raised my cup and we all clinked.

We parted company in considerably better mood than when we had met. I for one felt inspired by my idea and was totally fired up to staging the best ball the Dale had ever seen. It was almost a forgone conclusion that it would be a success given that Vera was so well loved and respected in the community.

Rebecca got home from school and I filled her in on what had happened. She too thought the ball was a great idea.

"Can I help you with it Mum? Please?"

"Course you can, darling, I'll absolutely be relying on you to fill me in on what's hot and what's not."

"Great! I can think of loads of ideas; when is it going to be?"

"That's a good question," I said. "I don't know. I guess it will depend on when the Town Hall is free."

"Well, I think either Christmas or in the middle of summer. Christmas would be my choice," she enthused.

"Oh, I'm not sure I could pull it out of the bag for Christmas, Becca, it's only a few months away. Besides, people don't have as much money to give away at Christmas."

"I suppose not," she said. "You see, I would never have thought of that, you are clever Mummy."

"Well, thank you Becca, what a nice thing to say."

"Can I go and watch TV now for a bit before tea?"

"Course," I said, and she ran off.

My God, what a difference. Out of all the things that had happened, all the traumas and the confusion that had engulfed me in my quest to be more interesting; the one thing I would not swap, was the 100% improvement in my relationship with my daughter. I wasn't quite sure what or how it had changed, but it definitely had.

We spent the evening quietly. Rebecca did her homework and then went to bed and I sat, notebook in hand, pondering ideas for 'The Vera Bailey Ball'.

I was deep in thought when the phone rang at 10.30pm and I was surprised to see Beryl's number come up. However, it wasn't Beryl's voice on the other end, it was Bill's.

"Hi Jo, I'm so sorry to ring so late," he said, sounding flustered.

"That's OK, Bill. Is everything all right?"

"I don't know," he said. "I wondered if you'd heard anything from Beryl. She hasn't come home yet and I'm starting to get worried."

"No, I'm sorry I haven't. Have you asked Jean?"

"Yes, I rang her before you. She hasn't spoken to her since she left her this morning. You don't think anything could have happened to her do you?"

"No, No," I said, trying to sound reassuring, "I'm sure where ever she is, she's fine. Jean did say she saw her heading to the pub, perhaps she had a few too many and decided to stay in town rather than drive back. By all accounts she was in a hell of a state this morning."

"I know, Jean told me. I can't understand why she's not answering her mobile though."

"Maybe her battery's flat? Happens to me all the time."

"Still, you'd think she could pick up a bloody phone to tell me she was OK, wouldn't you?"

"It is a bit inconsiderate, I grant you," I said. "Have you thought of ringing the police?"

"The police aren't interested unless someone's been missing for 24 hours. I have rung the hospitals though. They have my name in case anyone fitting her description is admitted."

"Oh Bill, you poor thing, I'm so sorry. I wish there was something I could suggest or do to help."

"No, it's fine. I guess I'll just have to wait it out. Stupid cow, this really is the last straw now, I've had enough of this."

"Look, I've got Rebecca here so I can't come out. But if you want to come over for a bit, just so you're not on your own, you know you're welcome to."

"Thanks Jo, that would be nice, but I can't, can I? I have to stay put in case the selfish bitch turns up. Anyway, I'd better get off, in case anyone's trying to ring."

"Well, if I hear anything, I'll ring you OK?"

"Yeah, thanks, I'll keep you posted. Bye then."

"Bye Bill."

Poor Bill. What the hell was Beryl up to now?

I didn't hear from him again that night and went to bed wondering where she could be. I felt sure nothing bad had happened to her. Although I hadn't said it to Bill, the most likely scenario was she'd picked up some guy in the pub and gone off for a night of illicit sex.

Or was I being a bit too harsh on her?

She had, unlike me, at least made it to Vera's court case and kicked off in public about it to boot. More than I had done.

No, perhaps she was just holed up somewhere trying to come to terms with whatever Vera's death had unleashed in her. I tried to ring her mobile, but there was no answer. I sent her a text anyway.

Beryl, Bill is really worried about you, please call him to let him know you're OK.

I didn't sleep particularly well, and waking up to the realisation that it was already Thursday did not make my mood any better. George and Philip would be descending on us this evening and I couldn't think of anything I would rather not do, than go through the charade of last weekend again.

If Bill hadn't been in the middle of a major Beryl drama, I would have been tempted to try and arrange another assignation at the barn for tonight. A little carnal pleasure might just have got me through the weekend.

I did ring him to see if he'd heard anything. He hadn't.

"The police said they would open a missing person's case from 12.00pm today, but there's not much they can do. Once I filled them in on the story they basically said that she's a grown woman and if she wants to disappear without telling anyone then she can."

"Well, I'm sure she's fine Bill. From what you've told me, it sounds like she's just having some time out. Maybe she just needs some space to get her head round everything that's been happening."

"I know, I have thought that too. But you'd think she could just text me or something?"

"Can they not give you any idea where she might be? I thought they could track mobiles or check credit cards and stuff like that."

"They can, but not till after 12.00pm."

"Well, maybe that will give you a bit more to go on. Come on, I'm sure it's all fine, honestly. Try to be positive, yeah?"

"I'm too bloody angry to stay positive, I just want to know what's happened that's all. Even if it was something really bad, I'd rather just know."

"Well, you know where I am if you need me," I said.

"Yeah, thanks, I'll let you know if I hear anything."

He hung up.

I could understand why he was starting to get worried.

I went to flower club, but more to see Jean and Caroline than to indulge in the delights of minimalist architectural sculpture using a spatula. Jean was of course totally preoccupied by Beryl's disappearance.

We dutifully completed our class, then went to the coffee shop.

"I am really, really worried about her now," said Jean. "Even if she hasn't got in touch with Bill, I thought she would at least call me."

"I'm sure she'll turn up," said Caroline. "Like the proverbial bad penny."

"You can't remember anything she said yesterday that could give us any clue to where she might be, Jean?" I asked.

"No, nothing, as I said she was ever so upset after the court case but we went our separate ways. I didn't want to leave her, but she insisted that she wanted to be on her own, and well you know Beryl, not much point in arguing with her once she's made up her mind.

"She had said last week that whilst we were down there she was going to go to the library to look up some stuff about her relations. She's been researching her family tree on and off for a few years now. But I can't see that being the reason she'd disappear, can you?"

"I wouldn't have thought so," I said.

"Bill was telling me, he'd filled you in on some of the stuff that's been going on," she continued.

I didn't know what to say.

"Well, he was telling me how worried he was about her, yes."

"It's OK Jo, you don't need to protect her any more. I think we're past the point of keeping this behind closed doors."

Silly women, did she not realise It wasn't Beryl I was protecting; it was Bill.

Poor Caroline was getting more confused as the conversation progressed.

"Have I missed something?" she asked. "It's just there seems to be a lot more going on here than Beryl getting upset yesterday."

"Just a bit," said Jean. "Jo can fill you in, but now I've got to go to a bloody costume meeting for the panto. We'll keep each other posted if we hear anything, yeah?"

"Course," I said.

We exchanged hugs and Jean left.

"So what's going on then, Jo?" asked Caroline.

I didn't think it was fair to Bill to tell her the whole sordid tale. So, I just told her about the antidepressants and the fact that Beryl had been troubled for quite some time but that no one knew why.

"God," she said. "Just goes to show, you never really know what's going on with anyone at all do you?"

Out of the mouths of babes, I thought. "No, you really don't," I said.

We finished our coffees and left.

For some reason, I decided to head to Bill's farm rather than going straight home. There had been so little I could do to help him in the last 24 hours it seemed. At least I could check he was ok and make sure he had food in the house or cook him a meal or something.

I pulled into the yard not knowing if he would be there, but was hopeful when I saw the Land Rover parked by the back door.

I knocked. There was no answer so I tried the handle and found it was open.

"Hello," I shouted. "Is anyone there? Bill, you about? It's me, Jo."

No reply.

I peeked my head round the door and peered into the gloom of the unlit kitchen.

I spotted him slumped over the kitchen table with what I recognised was the bottle of plum brandy we had all shared that first night. Poor love, no wonder he's fallen asleep: he must be exhausted. I should leave him in peace, but perhaps just find something to put round him. It was starting to get dark and I didn't want him to get cold.

I worried that putting the light on would disturb him, which made it hard to see and I couldn't spot anything to use, not even his coat. I went further into the kitchen being careful where I trod, but could find nothing.

I decided my good intentions were a waste of time if I ended up blundering into something and waking him anyway, so I quietly made for the door.

It was then I became aware of a soft dripping noise. Not a harsh noise like a tap dripping into the sink more a slow, soft drop like water through floorboards or from a ceiling. Oh dear, I bet the silly beggar has left the bath running or something.

I started to look round to see where it was coming from and then to my horror, I realised. All against the back wall, directly behind where Bill was sat, there was blood and what I guessed was bone and matter, splattered everywhere. I stood for a moment as my brain took in the scene and processed the information it had never had to process before.

I ran towards Bill, his face turned towards me. He can't be, I told myself, he just can't be. He did just look as though he was asleep. It was as I got closer that I realised that most of the back of his head was missing. His shot gun was between his legs, resting on the floor.

I didn't have the nerve to look for long, I knew he was dead; it didn't take a genius to work that one out.

"You stupid man!" I cried. "You stupid, stupid man. Why couldn't you have talked to me? You didn't need to do this!"

I went and sat down; I couldn't take in what had happened. It was just not real, it couldn't be. Why would he do such a thing?

I don't know how long I sat there: it could have been seconds, could have been minutes, could have been hours. I did eventually come back to the real world and tried to think what I should do next.

Police! Ring the police, that's the first thing to do.

I went outside and rang 999, then went back into the kitchen. I had an almost overwhelming urge to put the kettle on, but changed my mind when I saw it was covered in blood.

I glanced round the table where Bill lay; trying to see anything that would give me a clue as to why he would have felt things had got so bad that he had no other choice,

But there was nothing.

I sat back down to wait for the police and looked over at Bill's soft sweet face. All was so quiet and peaceful, with just the faint ticking of a clock somewhere to break the silence.

It wasn't long before the peace was shattered.

Are sirens absolutely necessary? Do we seriously need to alert the whole bloody town to new gossip so soon?

I headed to the kitchen door to let them in, then paused for a moment.

I went over to Bill and brushing his fringe away from his forehead, gave him a soft kiss.

"Goodbye, my dear lover."

I knew it would be the last time I would ever be alone with him.

The police took charge of the scene and of course, the first thing they did was put the bloody lights on. I had been fine in the gloom of the twilight lit kitchen. But as soon as the lights went on and the horrendous scene was there for me to see in all its wonderful, glorious Technicolor, I rushed out into the yard and threw up.

I couldn't go back in, so I gave my initial statement to a very sympathetic police officer in the back of his car. He said someone would come over to my house later to take a full statement.

They had offered to drive me home, but I convinced them that as it wasn't far, I would be fine. How I did, I have no idea. I had no recollection of pulling up at junctions or indicating to turn. I just had the vision of Bill, dead across the kitchen table, filling my eyes.

I got home, poured myself a large brandy, had a cigarette and waited for Rebecca to come home.

I briefly explained to her what had happened. She rushed over and gave me a huge hug.

"Oh Mummy, you poor, poor thing. Is there anything I can do for you, cup of tea?"

"No Becca. It's OK, I've hit the hard stuff I'm afraid." I waved the brandy glass.

"Don't blame you Mum, supposed to be very good for shock isn't it?"

"So they say, although I have never understood why."

"You could ring your dad and ask if he'd pick up a takeaway or something on his way home, I seriously don't feel like cooking now."

"Sure, course I can. I'll go and do it now."

She left me in the kitchen, sitting in my comfort chair, nursing my brandy.

She came back in a few minutes later. "Dad said that's fine, they'll be home in about an hour."

"Thanks Becca, you're a star."

She came and knelt in front of me, resting her hands on mine. It was such a sweet gesture, unimaginable a few weeks ago. I stroked her hair and smiled.

"So, did you know Beryl's husband well, Mum?"

Her question was innocent, I knew that, but still it triggered memories of the time we had spent together. The time I knew I would never have again.

I began to recall in my head the heart to heart we'd had just days before, trying desperately to remember anything he said that could have been a clue to what he could do. What did I miss? I should have seen how depressed he was, realised how low he had got. I should have been able to help him.

I wanted so much to cry but knew I couldn't.

It was absolutely crucial that no one ever found out about our relationship. There would be so much mud slung in the next few weeks, so many skeletons dragged out of closets for all to gape and gawp at.

I'd be dammed if I was going to let this man appear to be anything other than a devoted and loving husband. That was the least I could do for him.

"Mum, Mum, are you OK?"

"Sorry darling, I was miles away then. No, I didn't know him terribly well. Only like you know your friends' mums, I suppose," I said.

"Still Mum, it's very sad when someone thinks they don't have any other choice, isn't it?"

"Yes, darling, it is. It's tragic."

I couldn't take it any longer. I needed to get out of the room.

"Becca, if you don't mind, I'm just going to nip upstairs for a quick shower. You OK just watching telly for a bit or something?"

"Course I am."

She came and gave me another hug, then went off to watch TV.

I went upstairs, got in the shower, scrunched myself into a corner... and cried and cried and cried.

16
Secrets and Diaries

I got out of the shower and went downstairs just in time for George and Philip arriving. Becca had obviously filled them in over the phone on what had happened, because they each gave me a huge hug.

"There is just no let up for you at the moment, is there Jo," stated George sadly.

"No, it would seem not."

"Anyway, at least you don't have to worry about tea. We got an Indian, hope that's OK?"

I watched as they emptied the contents of the foil trays onto plates and felt decidedly sick.

"Err, actually George, I think I'll pass if you don't mind, a nice Rogan Josh is the last thing I want to see at the moment thank you."

I went and sat in my chair.

George looked at Philip puzzled.

"I don't understand, what have I done now?"

"Oh sweetie, it's my fault," he whispered. "I should have thought. Jo's just found someone that's blown their brains out. Curry, look at it, remind you of anything?"

"Oh shit, yes I see what you mean, bugger. Knew we should have gone for pizza. Sorry Jo."

"Yeah, so sorry Jo, just didn't think," said Philip.

"It's OK, it's not your fault. I'm not hungry anyway. I will however have a large glass of wine thanks."

George poured one and handed it to me.

"If you don't mind, I think I'll go through to the sitting room whilst you're all eating, I'll send Rebecca in."

I hadn't even made it through the hall when the doorbell rang. I opened it to a smartly dressed, tall, fair headed man, whom I guessed would be in his early fifties.

"Mrs Primm?"

I nodded.

"Detective Inspector Barns. Is this a convenient time for us to talk?"

"Yes, yes, by all means. Come in, please."

"Thank you."

I showed him into the sitting room.

"Can I get you anything: tea, coffee? I'd offer you a glass of wine or a beer, but I know you can't drink on duty can you?"

"No, that's right, a cup of tea would be very welcome though, if it's not too much trouble."

"I'll do it Mum," said Rebecca. "How do you take it?"

"Milk and two please, love. Thank you."

Just like Bill, I thought.

"This shouldn't take too long Mrs Primm. We've got your statement from the scene. What we're trying to piece together now is what led Mr South to take his own life. Can you help us with that at all?"

"I can only tell you what I know," I said.

So I did, I told the truth, the whole truth and nothing but the truth; well, except for the part about Bill and I enjoying some rather interesting outdoor pursuits. I didn't see that was any of his business.

I felt the wife-swapping, Beryl's disappearing act and the secret antidepressants, probably gave Bill more than enough motive for the police to see this as an open and shut case. He seemed satisfied when I'd recounted my tale.

"Very sad business," he said.

"Yes, yes it is. Bill was a good man. I'm sure he will be greatly missed."

"Had you known him long?"

"No, not really. I was more friends with Beryl his wife, we went to flower club together."

"But you went to the farm this afternoon, even though you knew Beryl was still missing?"

Did he know something? What's he getting at?

"Yes, I did," I said, trying to keep my composure.

"All Beryl's friends thought a lot of Bill, I just went to see if he needed anything. I knew how gutted he was about Beryl's disappearance; I just wanted to make sure he was OK. It's what we do round here Inspector, we look out for each other." My tone was a little sharp and a bit too defensive.

"It's OK Mrs Primm. I'm not implying that you did anything untoward. And just for the record I do come from round here, so I know exactly what people are like. I'm just trying to get a handle on why Bill, sorry, Mr South, did this."

His correction was too late for me not to pick up on it.

"Did you know Bill?" I asked.

"Yes, yes, I did," he said.

"I see."

There was an uncomfortable silence for a few moments.

"Look, Mrs Primm, I might as well come clean; Bill and I were at school together, I was best man at his wedding. This whole thing, well, it's just knocked me for six, I don't understand it. Christ, I only had a pint with him last week. It's just not like Bill, to be that, well that bloody bothered about anything."

"I'm so sorry, I had no idea."

He smiled a feeble smile and said, "It's OK, there's no way you could have known.

"I don't normally work up here, I'm usually based in Leeds."

So, is this Jean's contact, he must be the one that's been giving us the information on Vera's case?

"Right," I said, "so you know Jean and her husband then?"

"Yes, I do. Know most of the people round here actually."

"Well, that explains quite a lot. I did wonder why they'd assigned a detective inspector to a suicide, did seem a bit OTT."

"Yeah, well, I shouldn't even be part of the investigation, had to pull a lot of strings. If there had been even the vaguest hint of foul play they wouldn't have let me anywhere near. But as it is, it does genuinely look as though he'd just had enough."

"Look, are you sure I can't get you anything stronger than a cup of tea?"

"No, honestly, thank you, I'm fine. I should get going."

He stood up.

"Well, thank you for your time Mrs Primm, I'll let you know if we need anything further from you, but I doubt it." He headed to the door and turned.

"Just remember though, anything you do think of, no matter how small or trivial it might seem, please, please, give me a call. This card has my direct number and my mobile."

"I will, of course, but I think I have told you as much as I can."

"Oh, don't be too sure. You'd be amazed what people remember after traumatic events, sometimes weeks after."

"I'll have to take your word for that, thankfully I haven't had much experience of this kind of thing"

"That's why I'm also going to leave you the number for a counselling service. What you've had to deal with this afternoon, well, it can take time to get over. Not everyone's cup of tea counselling, but it's there if you need it."

"Thank you, that's very kind."

"Well, goodbye, Mrs Primm." He shook my hand.

"Goodbye Inspector."

I showed him out.

George appeared from the kitchen.

"That didn't take long. You OK?"

"Yes, I think so, well as OK as I can be I suppose. Nothing that a bit more red wine won't cure, at least temporarily anyway."

"Well, you go back through to the sitting room and I'll bring you a top up."

"Thanks."

He appeared back a few minutes later.

"Look," he said, "I've just had a word with Philip and he says he's quite happy to take Rebecca to rehearsals tonight. I'll stay here with you."

"You don't need to do that, George, I'm fine, honestly."

He sat beside me on the sofa and took my hand.

"I just don't think you should be on your own at the moment, that's all."

"Well, that's very sweet, but I will no doubt just drink too much red wine and fall asleep and you don't need to be here to hold my hand whilst I do that now do you?"

"I suppose not. Are you absolutely sure?"

"Absolutely."

"OK, then."

He gave me a kiss on the forehead.

True to my word, I downed the bottle of wine and went to bed, praying I would, one day, be able to fall asleep without the image of Bill's pale, peaceful face haunting me.

I rang Jean in the morning to see if she'd heard anything.

"I can't get over Bill," she said. "And God, *you*, Jo, you poor thing. Fancy being the one that found him."

"It was awful," I said. "I still can't get the image of him out of my head."

"I would have come to see you, but when I saw George at rehearsals he said you were going to try and get an early night."

"Yeah, I tried, but failed. But thanks for the thought anyway."

"What a mess, eh? Beryl won't even know yet, poor love, it's going to kill her when she finds out."

"Have you heard anything from the police?" I asked.

"No, nothing, it's like she's just vanished."

"Has anyone told the boys yet?" I asked.

"Yeah, Bill's sister's got them both down with her at the moment. They can't come back to the house just yet, police haven't finished with it."

"And what about the farm? Who's taking care of that?"

"Some of the other local farmers are doing the day to day stuff, but I'm guessing it'll need to be sold. Can't see Beryl keeping it on, assuming she ever comes back and neither of the boys wanted to go into farming."

"That's so sad," I said. "Bill loved that farm."

"I know, she might be my best friend, but she doesn't half make it hard to love her sometimes."

"Well, let me know if there's anything I can do to help, won't you?"

"Yeah, I will. Thanks Jo."

I put the phone down and made myself a cup of tea.

The events of the last 24 hours just didn't seem to be sinking in at all. How could our lives go from being normal to complete horror in such a short space of time?

Where the bloody hell was Beryl?

I tried to settle into my jobs for the day, but it was hard to concentrate on anything. I found myself daydreaming all the time, reliving the events of yesterday and trying to remember any small thing that would have made what Bill had done make some kind of sense.

When the morning post came I was surprised that there was a large handwritten envelope addressed to me. I hadn't been expecting anything and was quite excited as I opened it.

Once I had, I wished I hadn't. It was from Bill.

The police had said yesterday that is was unusual for suicides.not to leave a note. Not leaving a note was apparently more indicative of people making attempts at suicide as a cry for help; overdoses or wrist slashing being the preferred method for being found in time. A twelve bore shotgun, however, could not be seen as a half-hearted attempt.

Strange though, it had given me hope that perhaps Bill hadn't meant to kill himself and that the whole thing had been some kind of tragic gun cleaning accident. As I took out the contents of the envelope I realised with heavy heart that this was not the case.

There was a handwritten note, and an A4 foolscap hard backed book. The book looked old and as I flicked through the pages I realised it was some kind of journal.

I took it all through to the sitting room and sat down.

With tears uncontrollably welling up in my eyes, I read the note first.

My Dearest Jo,

This is the hardest thing I think I have ever had to do.

I know you will be angry with me and I also know that you will try in some way to blame yourself for what has happened.

Please believe me when I say nothing you have done or could do would have changed anything. Not because I don't care about you, but because sometimes things just can't be put right.

I am, however, sorry. Sorry that you have got messed up in all this and sorry because I am going to ask a favour of you that I have no right to ask as either a friend or a lover.

The book I have sent you, is Beryl's journal, she's kept it since she was a teenager. I came across it by accident the other night.

My mate Paul Barnes, had suggested I go through her stuff to see if I could find any clues as to where she might be, and there it was tucked in her knicker drawer where she always kept it. I'd forgotten she even had it.

I knew she wrote in it from time to time, but I'd never had any inclination to read it. It contained her private thoughts and I genuinely believed that she was entitled to them.

I'd meant to read the last couple of pages and I wish to God now that I had. But I didn't, I read the whole thing, and well, once you've read it, I think you'll understand.

I have no idea if Beryl will ever come back and I have no idea who will be first in the house when I'm gone. But I do know that no one else can find this book. The pain it would cause so many people just doesn't bear thinking about.

That's my final straw.

It's not the lies or the being unfaithful that hurts the most, it's the fact that she never for one moment thought to confide in me. Beryl has some real problems, problems that as the man that loved her more than anything in the world, she wouldn't even share with me. All these years and she never trusted I would care for her enough to want to try and help.

Sometimes you can know too much about a person and if you love them with all your heart, their faults and failings can be too overwhelming to come to terms with.

I have sent the book to you, because I trust you. I was never meant to know the secrets it reveals and they are secrets that must still be kept.

You are a remarkable and wonderful person Jo and I want you to know I have no regrets about the time we spent together. You have been a true friend and I thank you for that.

I know I have put you in a terrible position but I'm afraid I could think of no one I would rather speak my final thoughts to than you.

If Beryl does ever come back, don't tell her anything about my letter or the journal. I am not just trusting you with my last wishes, I am trusting you with the future happiness of my family as well.

The final favour I ask is that you burn the book. I don't care if Beryl spends the rest of her life wondering what happened to it, I don't want the boys ever finding out what's in it.

Well, I suppose that covers everything. This must be the longest letter I have ever written, stalling for time, maybe, but I have to go now. I want to make sure it catches the last post tonight.

Forgive me Jo and thank you.

Bill xx

I could hear his voice in my head as I read his words, somehow it made him seem alive again. I must have re-read it ten times.

I looked at the scratty A4 book. The book that had contained information so damning it had caused a man to take his own life. What on earth could she have done that was so bad?

I was almost afraid to read it. I knew that once I'd turned the first page, I was committing myself to being eternally linked with a family barely knew.

God, why me? Why not Jean, Bill? She was Beryl's best friend after all. She'd known Bill for years and to be honest would know most of what was in the bloody book anyway.

No, Bill was my friend and he had asked me to do it, so I did.

The first thing I realised was that it was not, as such a diary; it was more an events record of things that had happened in Beryl's life.

I started at the beginning and read through the entries that must have begun in her teens. It was all fairly predictable stuff: first kiss, exam results, when she lost her virginity, nothing controversial at all.

I persevered.

I got to when she met Bill and how happy she was, she'd even written in it on her wedding day. The first entry that made me take notice was one shortly after they had got married. It read:

> Told Bill about my extra-curricular activities. He got really upset. Explained to him that it was nothing to worry about and that I still loved him, but he didn't seem to get it. Not sure I do. Why can't I just be like other woman and be happy with what I've got?

I read a few pages forward.

> Been to the docs again. They say Bill has a low sperm count, it's not impossible for us to have children, but it will make it a lot harder. Poor Bill, he thinks he's failed me. Really feeling the urge to go on one of my adventures, wish I could persuade Bill to come too, would be so much easier if he would join in.

Then there was the first bomb shell:

> *I am pregnant! Trouble is I know it's not Bill's. Think it was the fireman I had it away with at a swapping party last month. Can't tell Bill, know he would be gutted. Do I get rid or keep it and pretend it's his? Don't think I could kill a baby. Bloody hell!*

I read on.

> *Couldn't go through with it; have decided to brave it out. Told Bill and he's over the moon. Says, "Just goes to show, what do these bloody doctors know anyway?" Poor sod. I hope to God he never finds out. Feel like a complete shit. Must stop the extra activities, it's not fair. Especially now I am going to be a mum.*

To be fair to her from the next lot of entries she seems to have packed in her affairs. But then they started up again when her eldest child got to about three years old.

> *My urge is back and I can't seem to get rid of it. Bill has begged me not to but am going to a swapping party this weekend. Can't bloody wait!*

A month later.

> *Don't fucking believe it! I've done it again, managed to get bloody pregnant. I knew that bastard was lying when he said he'd had the snip. Guess I'll have to go through it all again. Need to have sex with Bill PDQ or he'll guess it's not his.*

I couldn't get to grips with Beryl from her diary at all. It was beginning to seem as though her affairs were almost an addiction, something she couldn't help, even though she did try.

I read on through a fairly uneventful few years. The boys' birthdays, some rather sordid descriptions of her affairs, her delight in getting Bill to join her in them so she didn't need to feel guilty anymore. And then another shocker.

Mum's, dying, docs say she only has a few days left. Went to see her and the wicked old cow finally admitted who my dad was. Turns out he was a bloody bigamist. Had another wife in London. Seems he didn't leave us like she told us. He only went and bloody killed himself, something to do with beating up his pregnant wife and killing his baby. Thought I'd try to get her to finally own up to knowing what 'Uncle Ben' had been up to for all those years, but she wouldn't. Hope she rots in hell. God, what a family.

Hell, fancy Beryl's dad killing himself like Vera's husband did, what a coincidence and who the hell was Uncle Ben? I hoped to God the reference didn't mean what I thought it might.

I read on.

Went to see the doc today about getting some happy pills. Am hoping they might help with my wandering urges. I'm sure it's all down to hormones. Have promised Bill I'll cut it down from now on. Besides, I'm no spring chicken any more. I don't seem to have the pulling power that I did. Some of the old dogs I've ended up with recently would make you gag if you saw them in daylight!

I continued on, reading page after page about her indiscretions, Bill's refusal to be part of it anymore and her desperate attempts to fight what was obviously an addiction.

On a more positive note her determination to get to the bottom of her family history was impressive.

Been doing some online research into my family history, it's amazing what you can get hold of on the internet. Got Mum and Dad's marriage certificate, but can't find anything yet on the other one. Sly bugger, bet he used a different name. Anyway will keep looking. Seems he was in the army. Quite heroic by all accounts, was in Germany and everything. Wonder what went wrong with him?

I frantically read through the book trying to find any other mention of her family and then there it was, her entry on the day of Vera's funeral.

Today we buried Vera Bailey, who it turns out was married to my dad. I went to see the vicar after and he told me his name. He hadn't changed it. I wonder if Vera ever knew. Don't think she did.

I read on. There was another entry a few days later.

Update on the dad story, seems he married Vera in Germany that's why I couldn't get hold of the certificate. Tracked it down through military records. Never came back to Mum and me, left us high and dry. Quite glad really knowing what I do now; still, poor old sod obviously had a hell of a time of it. I am so angry that I will never get chance to talk to Vera about it. God knows what she would have made of it all, but at least she might have been able to tell me something. Could kill that bloody lass.

Next entry.

Feel like my head is going to explode. Can't get it round the whole Vera thing, she could have been my mum and not that evil cow. My life could have been so different. Have told Bill I need to go away for a night or two. I've told him where and he's gone off on one again. Wish he'd just leave me alone. He's like a fucking puppy sometimes that I just want to kick.

There was just one other entry after that.

Going to Vera's court hearing tomorrow, I hope to God that girl gets banged up, otherwise others will have to see justice is done.

I sat and tried to digest the complexity of the information I had just read. I was feeling thankful that the worst I had to contend with was a devoted dad that just happened to be gay.

I re-read her last entry. Surely she wouldn't be stupid enough to take the law into her own hands, would she? No, I told myself, too many episodes of Agatha Christie, Jo. Don't get carried away. This was the Yorkshire Dales not Midsomer.

I took the letter and the journal to my room and hid them under my mattress. I would burn the journal later, after everyone else had gone to bed. Bill's letter I would keep forever.

I passed the time doing nothing I could consciously re-member. I seemed to be living two different lives: the one in reality and the one going on in my head.

To give them their dues, George and Philip were being brilliant doing all the cooking and the tidying.

They had suggested that we all went out on the Friday night, but I just wasn't in the mood. I asked if they could take Rebecca though. I didn't want her being dragged down by all this, so they went out for an early dinner and then to see a film.

I waved them off looking out the sitting room window, then glanced across to the hill where Bill's barn was. I'd never realised I could see it from here till now. I drifted off for a moment and allowed myself to remember that breath-taking night. A wave of sadness washing over me as I realised I would never be able to look at that view without remember-ing the wonderful man I shared such special times with.

Then I noticed something. It was lit.

There was definitely a soft light shining through the small slatted windows. But it was disused; Bill had told me that, that's why he'd chosen it.

So, who the hell was in it now and what the hell were they up to?

I felt angry. I couldn't bear the idea that someone was on his land, doing God knows what. They had no right to be there.

I decided to ring Detective Inspector Barnes.

"I'm sorry," I said. "I didn't know who else to call. Should I have just rung the local police?"

"No, it's fine," he said. "I'm glad you told me. Funnily enough, I was going to call you. There's been a development in Beryl's case. It seems that Gemma Smith, that's the girl who was up in court for attacking Vera, well, she hasn't been seen since late on Wednesday afternoon. She hasn't checked in with her parole officer or been to the drug clinic, and her parents can't get hold of her either. The police down there were treating her as an absconder."

"Oh my God," I said. "Do you think the two are connected?"

"I honestly don't know, Mrs Primm. Seems a bit too much of a coincidence for them not to be, don't you think?"

"Please, Detective Inspector, call me Jo."

"Paul, Jo. Call me Paul."

"OK, Paul. So what happens now?"

"Well, the boys down there are starting to make enquiries in and around the pub where Beryl was last seen, seems that Gemma Smith might have also gone in there after the hearing. Is there anything else you know that could give us an idea of where to start?"

There was a moment's silence.

"Paul," I said. "Are you far from here? I think I need to show you something. But please, this is incredibly sensitive. I need to talk to you as Bill's friend not as a police officer. It might be better if you came alone."

"All sounds a bit strange and well, frankly, very unorthodox, but yes OK, I'm just in the village at the moment. I'm staying up here for a few days tying up loose ends. I can be there in about 15mins."

"Thank you."

True to his word he arrived 15 minutes later alone.

"It's all a bit cloak and dagger this Mrs Primm, sorry I mean Jo."

We moved across to the sofas.

"I know, I'm sorry. But before I show you this Paul, I have to have your solemn promise that you will not tell another living soul what you are about to read."

"Go on," he said. His voice was filled with scepticism.

I took Beryl's diary and Bill's note from the bag I had retrieved from under my mattress.

"I got these in the post this morning." I clasped them to my chest.

"They're from Bill. One is well," I paused. "Well, I suppose you would say it's a suicide note. The other is Beryl's diary."

"I see," he said. His look was calm but pensive.

"I am in a complete dilemma," I pleaded. "I don't know what to do. He has asked me as his dying wish to destroy this book. The problem is I think some of the stuff in it could explain why Beryl and this girl have gone missing."

"And the note?" he questioned.

"The note is just asking me to protect his family by destroying the book."

"May I see them?"

I hesitated. "You can see the diary, but please, I'd rather not show you the note."

"Jo, I understand that you are trying to protect Bill, but please trust me. I promise, whatever is in it will go no further."

I handed them over to him and directed him to the passages in the book that told of Beryl's pregnancies, then to the sections about her family and then finally to the entries about the court case. He then read the note.

Showing no expression, he handed them back to me.

"And you seriously think Beryl might have done something to this girl?" he said.

"I do," I urged. "You must have heard about what happened in the court room."

"Well, by all accounts she was more than a little upset."

"What are you going to do?"

"I don't know," he sighed. "But that glass of wine would go down a treat right about now."

"I thought you couldn't drink on duty?"

"I'm not on duty."

"Fair enough then, if you'd rather, we do have brandy. I realise this is just as much of a shock to you as it was to me."

"No, wine's fine. Thank you."

I wandered into the kitchen and poured a glass of red and took it through.

"Sorry," I said. "I should have asked which you prefer."

"Red's fine, I prefer red."

He had gone quiet and sombre, I could tell he was mulling over what he had read and what to do about it.

"You know, I should be taking those items in as evidence, don't you?"

"Yes, I do, but please, you've read his note you know that's the last thing he wanted."

"This is quite a dilemma for me too you know. I can't do anything to move this investigation on Jo, if I can't produce these items to back up your theory."

"No, I know that," I said. "But there is one thing you're forgetting."

"Really? What?"

"That," I said, pointing out of the window.

He came and stood beside me

"What?"

"That," I said, "that's Bill's barn. The one I told you about on the phone. Don't you think it's a bit strange that it's lit?"

"And you think that's where Beryl is?"

"I don't know. It could be."

"And you think I should go and check it out?"

"No," I said. "I think *we* should go and check it out."

17
Grim and Bear It

It took me several minutes to persuade Paul that it would be a good idea to walk up to the barn.

"Let's face it," I said finally. "If I'm wrong the worst we will encounter is a couple of walkers dossing in the barn for the night."

"And if you're right," he said. "Have you thought about that?"

"No, I haven't, but I don't think either of us could live with ourselves if we didn't check it out, do you?"

"Oh, alright. You do realise though that this is strictly against regulations. I should be calling for backup not romping up a hillside with a, well a...." he paused.

"Yes?" I said. "What were you going to say? With a what, with a delusional middle aged woman you mean. You cheeky sod."

"No, of course not. What I was going to say was 'with an inexperienced member of the public.'"

"Oh, right, sorry. Well, shall we get on then?"

We walked down the drive and crossed over the road to start heading up the short track that led to the barn. The air was cold with a definite frost hanging in the mist that was starting to fall into the valley.

So much had happened since I had first walked this path. The first time my heart had been pounding with anticipation and lust at the prospect of meeting my lovely Bill. This time it was pounding with excitement and fear that I would meet God knows what.

As we approached, we could see the door was slightly open. The light was not as welcoming as it had been on my first visit; this light was hidden and minimal. I had rather hoped we would hear the chattering of a couple of campers about to settle down to their evening meal, but all you could hear was the frosty wind and the odd hoot of a barn owl.

Paul put his fingers to his lips.

"Keep quiet, I'll go in first, see what's what. We don't know who could be inside," he whispered.

I nodded and cautiously followed a few steps behind.

He peeked his head round the door and with a short gasp of breath immediately pulled it out again.

"What! What is it?" I whispered.

"Don't go in there Jo, you don't want to see."

"What is it, is it Beryl?" I urged.

"Yes, yes it is," he said. "But I'm afraid she's dead."

"What, no, she can't be. Let me see."

"No," he said firmly. "You wait here. I need to call this in."

He left me standing outside. I could hear him talking on his mobile but couldn't make out what he was saying. My need to know was becoming overpowering. Whatever was in there it couldn't be worse than what I had seen the other day, surely? So I went in.

The light was very dim and it took a moment for my eyes to adjust. When they did, I let out a sharp gasp. Beryl had hung herself from the rafter of the hayloft where Bill and I had had sex.

Oh, this is just bloody brilliant. Of all the things to do this had to be the most senseless and ridiculous of all. My God did she know about us? Is that why she chose this barn and that spot?

"I thought I told you to stay outside!" Paul snapped.

"Yes, I know, but I couldn't," I snapped back. "Shouldn't we try and do something; I mean she could still be alive couldn't she?" I rushed over to the loft and began to climb the ladder.

"No Jo, you can't, she's definitely dead, trust me, I know. We need to wait for the SOC guys to get here. Wait outside, please!"

"But can't we at least cut her down? It seems wrong to just leave her there!"

"I'm afraid not. Now please, outside."

"All right, All right, I'm going, seems a bit bloody callous if you ask me."

"Well, I didn't. Out!"

Bloody men, I thought as I headed for the door then stopped.

"Paul, did you hear that!" I exclaimed. "My God she is still alive, I heard a groan, I definitely heard a groan, now cut her down, cut her down!" I yelled.

He turned looking panicked, "What? No, I didn't hear anything and she's definitely not alive, now shut up and let me listen."

We stood in silence. Then there it was again. A barely imperceptible, but nevertheless real, moan.

"It's coming from the back of the barn," said Paul.

We rushed to where the noise was coming from to find a pile of empty sacks and rags.

They moved.

I jumped back, but Paul knelt down and very carefully pulled them back.

Looking half frozen, dressed in only a short skirt and a thin blouse, was a young girl.

Her hands and feet were bound and starting to go blue with cold. She had no shoes or tights on and her mouth was covered by Gaffer tape.

I don't think I have ever seen anyone look so pale and close to death. Not because she was injured, but because she had lost any hope of living. She was absolutely terrified and started to try and shuffle back away from us

"It's alright love," Paul said calmly. "I'm a police officer, I'm here to help you."

He turned to me.

"Jo, go and have a hunt round for anything you can find that might help warm her up will you? She's in very serious danger of getting hypothermia."

"Yes, right, of course."

"Now, stay calm sweetheart, we're going to get you sorted. I'm going to take this tape off your mouth now. I'll be as gentle as I can but it might sting a bit, OK?"

The girl nodded, tears now streaming down her face.

"OK, here we go," he said. "Are you hurt anywhere?"

She shook her head as he gently removed the tape.

"Thank God," she cried. "Thank God someone has found me. I thought I was going to die up here."

"Well, you're all right now," said Paul. "Are you Gemma Smith?"

"Yes, yes I am. How did you know?"

"Oh, just a shrewd guess. Now let's see about getting your arms and legs free shall we?"

He untied her hands and feet and began rubbing them between his hands.

"Just as well we got here when we did, Gemma. You could have frozen to death up here if we'd been a few hours later. You have this lady to thank for that. Reckon she may well have saved your life."

"Yes, but not Beryl's though," I said.

"What, what do you mean not Beryl's? Where is she, where's Beryl?" cried Gemma. I was shocked that her voice was concerned rather than scared.

"She didn't do it, did she? She didn't kill herself?"

"I'm afraid she has, love," said Paul gently.

She broke down sobbing. "I told her not to. I told her we could sort it."

"Well, don't worry about it now. We need to get you out of here. Do you think you can walk?"

"I, I don't know."

She stood up and immediately fell down again.

"I've got these," I said, handing him a couple of old coats and a blanket which Bill had left in the hayloft from when we had been there together. There was also an old brazier that I'd filled with sticks and straw.

"Don't suppose you have any matches do you?" I asked.

He reached into his pocket and handed me a lighter.

"Always the boy scout," he smiled softly.

He took the coats and blanket and wrapped them around the girl, still rubbing her hands and feet to try and get her circulation going. She looked so pale.

I moved the brazier closer and lit it, then began to look around for more fuel all the while trying to avoid catching the eye of the still swinging Beryl.

"I'm going to get her down," said Paul. "Shouldn't really, but now we've found the girl I think we can spare her the trauma of having to look at that whilst we wait for the ambulance, can't we?"

Charming, but it was alright for me to have to!

I helped him lower Beryl's body to the ground and then found some sackcloth to cover her with. I know I should have felt sad for her, but I just couldn't. After everything she had put Bill through I just couldn't find it in my heart to feel anything. Well, not then anyway.

Paul rang his team and told them to send a second ambulance.

He then sat with Gemma whilst we waited for them to come. I could hear his voice talking to her softly and calmly, reassuring her that everything was going to be all right. She was obviously in shock and in no fit state to tell us much.

I busied myself with finding more bits of wood for the fire and further explored the barn where Beryl had obviously been holed up for the last few days.

There were several bottles of water and some biscuits which I immediately passed to Paul so that Gemma could have a drink and something to eat.

A bucket which had obviously been used as a toilet but that was thankfully empty.

I could just imagine Beryl tidying up before she did the deed, making sure that there were no loose ends. Well, apart from Gemma anyway.

And what about Gemma? If Beryl had bound her and then killed herself how was she expecting the girl to get away? Or perhaps she hadn't meant for her to escape: perhaps she'd intended to kill her, but couldn't go through with it so had killed herself instead.

We would, I feared, never find out.

I carried on with my search and even found Beryl's handbag. It made me pause and contemplate what to do next.

As every woman knows a handbag is sacrosanct and should never knowingly be interfered with. To delve into someone else's handbag is like reading someone else's diary or sleeping with another woman's husband.

Bugger it, might as well go for the hat-trick. Besides, there was an envelope sticking out the top of it. I turned my back to

Paul so he couldn't see what I was doing and took the envelope out of Beryl's bag. It was addressed to Bill.

Could this be Beryl's suicide note?

My immediate reaction should have been to take it to Paul, but I didn't. I slipped it very quickly into my coat pocket. A few minutes later there was the sound of sirens and the police and the ambulances arrived.

Paul went to speak to his colleagues and then came back over to me.

"They'll take it from here. I'll walk you back up to the house and pick up my car. I'll need to head back into work now."

"Yes, fine, OK," I said.

We watched the ambulances speed off and left a couple of officers inside the barn taking photographs.

"They'll seal it off," said Paul. "You know, put tape round it so no one goes in."

"Right."

We walked back up to the house in silence.

"I'll come in for a minute if that's all right," he said. "I think you could do with a stiff drink."

We got in and I went and sat in the sitting room. The others weren't back yet and the silence of the house seemed daunting. Being left alone with the images I had in my head was frightening.

Paul came into the room carrying a large glass of brandy.

"There you go. Get that down you."

"Thanks," I said, "how did you know where to find it?"

"Ah well, I'm not a detective inspector for nothing you know."

He came and sat down.

"So how are you doing?"

"I don't think I know," I said. "You must see things like this every day in your job. Do you ever get used to it?"

"Yes and no," he said. "Some things hit you harder than others, crimes involving children I think are always the worst, or people you know."

"Well, I don't know how you do it. I now have two images in my head that I doubt I will ever be able to forget."

"Well, you will," he said, giving my hand a reassuring pat. "You should be proud of yourself. If you hadn't noticed what you did and followed your gut instinct that girl could well have died."

"That girl," I said, "is the reason that all this mess had been caused. Does she realise that she's now responsible for the death of three people?"

"Oh now, come on Jo, that's a bit harsh isn't it? I mean she's definitely no angel, but do you honestly think she wanted these people to end up dead?"

"How should I know?" I yelled. "Oh, ignore me. I don't know what I'm saying or thinking at the moment."

"Well, I think you'll find she'll be just as traumatised by all this as you are. Trust me, this kid is no hard-nosed criminal. She's just a girl that got mixed up with the wrong sort."

"Yeah, well, we all make our choices in life. It just seems like some of us have to end up living with the consequences of other people's mistakes."

"Quite possibly true, but none of us are perfect now are we?"

"Hmm…" I took a slug of my brandy.

"Well, I need to get going. I'll be in touch. There won't be much else happening tonight. We'll let the girl get a good night's rest and then go in tomorrow morning to interview her. I'll let you know what I can if you would like me to."

"Yes, absolutely," I said. "Thank you. Paul, should I ring Jean? She needs to know, Beryl was her best friend."

"No, it's OK, I'll sort that. I'll call in to see her on my way back to the station. You try and get some rest."

I stood up to show him out.

"Night Jo, try and get some sleep."

"Yes I will, bye."

I shut the door and went straight to my coat pocket to find the letter from Beryl.

Taking another sip of brandy I opened it.

It was surprisingly short.

My Dear Bill,

I realise this isn't the ending for us that you had wished for, but as per usual, I have got myself into a right pickle and to be frank, don't have a fucking clue how to get out of it.

I took the girl honestly thinking I wanted to kill her, but the truth is as my whole life is proof of – I am a coward. True to form, my love, I shall leave you to pick up the pieces of the mess I am about to leave behind.

I know how much you love me and I know that as long as I am around you would always try and find a way to make things better. Trouble is Bill, some things just can't be mended. You're such a good man and deserve far better than me. You have put up with my strange ways for long enough and it's time you didn't have to anymore.

Tell the boys I love them and to be strong and that I honestly never meant to hurt anyone.

Forgive me using the barn. It's just, well, we had such special times up here when we were courting and I wanted the last thing I saw to be something that reminded me of happier days.

I have no idea when or if I will be found. I have told Gemma that her fate is in the hands of God. If she is destined to live then she will and if not she will die.

*To my mind that thought should be sentence
enough for anyone.*

    Beryl x

So that's it, I thought sadly. Beryl and Bill are both dead.

I have to confess I felt a slight pang of hurt on reading that Bill had also spent time with Beryl in the barn. Had he just been using me to try and rekindle the memories of the happier times he had shared with the woman he truly loved?

What a complete and utter bloody mess; how ridiculous that two loving and caring people could end up in such a tragedy.

Two suicide notes that would never be read by either of the people they were intended for. Two boys left without either parent to explain to them what the hell had gone on, And me stuck somewhere in the middle, trying to make sense of how the hell I could be involved in such a sorry story in the first place. I mean, for crying out loud, all I did was join a bloody flower arranging class!

I sat and finished my brandy preparing for the others to return, knowing I would have to retell the awful events of the night.

When they did get back they already knew something had gone on. Two ambulances and police cars, high-speeding through our small country lanes, was not a day to day occurrence and word had already hit the village that something major had happened.

I didn't want Rebecca to get involved, so I waited until she'd gone to bed before I recounted the whole sorry tale to George and Philip.

They were appropriately shocked by the further revelations of the Beryl and Bill saga.

"It's like something out of Thomas Hardy!" exclaimed Philip.

"I hardly think Beryl could be described as *Tess of the d'Urbervilles*, do you?" I replied.

"No, but you have to admit it's not the kind of thing you expect round here now is it?" said George.

"That poor girl," said Philip. "Imagine what an ordeal she's been through."

"That poor girl," I said, "is the cause of this whole sodding thing."

"Well, one thing's for sure, Jo. You've got yourself embroiled in a real old mess. I can't imagine how you must be feeling," said George.

"Bloody knackered," I said. "Like my head's been hit with a sledgehammer."

"Well, you just tell us what you need us to do and we'll do it. Won't we Philip?"

"Absolutely," came the firm response.

I looked at them both with warmth of feeling that was heartfelt. How quickly they had become a consolidated, loving and supportive couple. I knew they meant every word. How lucky I was, I thought.

"Well, I think what I need right now, is a bath. So if you'll both excuse me."

"Of course," said George. "Give me a shout if you need anything."

"I will. Thanks."

He came over and gave me a big hug, closely followed by Philip,

I went and had a long soak and tried to get my thoughts about the last 48 hours into some kind of order. I didn't succeed.

When I came back downstairs George and Philip were in the sitting room, talking in hushed voices. They stopped when I walked in.

"Not interrupting anything am I?"

"No, not all," said George. "We were in fact, just talking about you."

"Really?" I said. "Well, at one time I would have said that would make for brief conversation, but nowadays - hell who knows!"

I plonked myself heavily on the sofa.

"Look," said George, "I know you're going to say you're fine, but I've decided I'm going to take next week off work."

"What!" I shouted, jumping to my feet. "Why on earth would you do that? You never take time off work, I mean for God's sake George you only took an afternoon off when Rebecca was born!"

"I know, I know, but this is different. We think you're going to need a lot of support with all this, even if it's just to help out with Rebecca. And well, in view of how brilliant you've been about Philip and me; we do think it's the least we can do."

"Oh George, there's no need. I'm fine, honestly," I insisted.

"I knew you'd say that, but I'm afraid I won't take no for an answer. Philip's going to stay for the weekend and then go back to town on Monday, if it's OK with you he'll come back on Thursday as usual."

"It's the right thing to do, Jo," said Philip. "Please let us help you."

"Well, it appears you have already decided. So I guess there is not much I can do about it."

"Good, now come and sit down," George said, patting the seat next to him.

"I have to be honest, I've never had to deal with anything like this before. I'm not sure I know what to do. Do you want to talk about anything?"

"Yes, talking is definitely supposed to help, do you want to talk about it Jo?" said Philip with sincerity almost bursting out of his pore perfect skin.

Bless them, their faces were so earnest to help. Yet they were totally clueless as to what this had fundamentally all been about and I couldn't tell them. I needed to escape.

"I think I might just go up to bed."

"Yes, fine, well rest is always good in these situations as well," said George. "You probably know best."

"Oh, I think if that were the case, I wouldn't be in this situation now, would I George?"

"No, well, you know what I mean."

"Yes, I do, and you're very sweet, you're both very sweet. Thank you."

I stood up to leave.

"Good night then."

"Good night Jo," said George.

"Hope you sleep," said Philip.

"So do I," I said and left them to it.

I don't think it could be unexpected that I didn't sleep. Too many questions, too many images and too little explanation.

I had considered in the small hours of the morning whether I should just tell George that I wanted to move; to leave everything behind us and start afresh somewhere, with Philip in tow, obviously.

But then I remembered Vera, the lovely lady who had unintentionally caused this train of events to happen in the first place.

No, it wouldn't be right, especially with what had happened to Bill and Beryl. It was more important than ever that I made something positive come out of this wreck of events.

Paul rang me later that day and filled me in a little on what had happened to Beryl and Gemma at the barn.

Beryl had apparently followed her into the bar after the hearing and befriended her. She subsequently plied her with enough drink to fell a small pony and then told her she would give her a lift home. She didn't of course, she took her up to the barn where she proceeded to bind and gag her whilst the poor girl was unconscious from the booze. She'd then driven back down to the main road and parked her car in a walkers' car park.

"She didn't hurt her, though," said Paul. "She talked to her, told her all sorts of stuff about her life and did a fair bit of shouting at her, but by all accounts Gemma never felt afraid for her life."

"No, well, I don't think any of us would consider Beryl to be the murdering type, if there is such a thing."

"Never underestimate what people are capable of Jo, you push someone over the edge and you'd be horrified by what they are capable of doing."

"Yes, well, I suppose, you'd know," I said. "Being in your line of work I mean, not you personally."

He laughed.

"No, I do know what you mean."

"Anyway, the girl is going to be fine. They are letting her out of hospital tomorrow, her mum and dad are coming to get her.

"Whether Beryl intended it or not I think Gemma will be a rather different person from now on. Sometimes being able to directly see the impact you have on other people's lives can make a tremendous difference to how you behave. But I'm guessing you already know that."

"Me? Hardly! I was doing fine until I joined that bloody flower club now I have three dead friends, a broken marriage and a nicotine addiction."

"Well, if you put it like that..."

"Anyway, thanks for keeping me posted, if you need me for anything else, you know where I am."

"Yes, I do. And thank you, without your help and Bill's faith in you we could have been counting four people dead and not three. Just remember that."

"Yes, I will. Bye."

18
The Show Must Go On

The next few weeks were spent in a bizarre mix of funerals and panto dress rehearsals. Talk about art imitating life!

Beryl and Bill's funeral was a joint affair. It was decided that despite their problems, in truth, they did love each other and they deserved to rest in peace together. It had of course been a complete contrast to Vera's funeral: theirs being a commiseration of what should have been rather than a remembrance of what had.

I made a promise to myself that I would take Bill a white rose each week in reminiscence of the light and hope he had brought into my life. Beryl – I would occasionally relocate another chap's urn and replace it for Bill's: so she could still have a change now and again.

Although no one would have imagined it, panto proved to be the perfect antidote to the trauma that we had all gone through.

I dutifully took my place backstage as promised and watched as Philip took the world of village theatre by storm. He was every bit as good as I guessed he might be and quite deservedly stole the show.

However, the surprise of the night was yet to come.

We had all been invited back to Imelda's for the after show party. I hadn't wanted to go, but it seemed a bit churlish to put a downer on everybody else's triumph.

It was a nice enough do, plenty of champagne and over catered canapés, but quite jolly.

I passed the evening chatting to people and being sought out in conversation because of the part I had played in Bill and Beryl's tragedy. I just said I would rather not talk about it and quickly changed the subject.

As the night drew on, it was time for Imelda to give her director's speech which was the dutiful mix of thanks and self-praise synonymous, I was told, with such affairs.

It was when she was delivering her speech about Philip that things took an unexpected twist.

"My darlings," she began. "It is rare in our humble little village that we come across a talent the magnitude of Mr Philip Darwin. The fact that he saw fit to join our merry band is truly amazing. The fact that he did so at a time when we were desperately in need, shows his character of true kindness and selflessness. Ladies and Gentlemen, I would ask you to raise a glass to our very own 'Dame Dotty Trot'."

A cheer went up, followed by a chorus of "To Dame Dotty Trot!"

"Speech, speech," a chant of voices yelled.

"Thank you, thank you all, so much," came Philip's soft understated voice.

"I have had a wonderful time working with you all and dare I say, would even come back next year if I was asked."

A resounding cheer went up from the guests.

"However," he continued, "I would not have been able to give such a convincing and authentic performance if I hadn't had the support of my partner and the love of my life George Primm. George, I love you." He raised his glass and looked across at George.

The room immediately fell silent and all eyes turned to where George was standing.

Oh shit, he really, really shouldn't have said that.

To my absolute astonishment, George took a low bow, blew Philip a kiss and shouted, "I love you too!"

Still silence, then to my utter amazement another resounding cheer went up and all was well.

I felt a sharp dig in my ribs. It was Jean.

"Well, that does explain a lot," she whispered. "You are a sly one Jo."

"Not sly, Jean. Just careful."

I had to find Rebecca, God knows what she thinks of all this.

I needn't have worried; she was standing with Philip and George chatting away as if nothing had happened.

"Becca, can I just have a quick word?" I gestured.

"Course Mum, are you having a lovely time? I am, isn't it a brilliant party?"

"Yes, darling, it is. I just wanted to talk to you about Daddy."

"Oh, you mean about him and Philip? Don't worry Mum, it's cool. I've known for ages. They're not exactly good at hiding it are they?"

"And you don't mind? You're OK with it?"

"Mum - you and Dad have never been so happy together, I think it's great and Philip is wonderful. We just need to get you fixed up with someone now don't we?" she gave me a cheeky wink and a hug.

"And everyone else, you're not going to get a hard time at school or anything?"

"Are you kidding, do you have any idea how much cred this will give me! Philip was the dame for goodness sakes, how cool can it get? Now stop worrying and have a good time." She disappeared off to find her friends and left me stood in the middle of a party wondering what on earth people must think of me.

I managed to get through the evening by hiding in corners to avoid awkward conversations. When Peter Sullivan the head of the Town Council came over to talk to me, I felt sure my number was up and that I would be told I was to be run out of town.

"Evening, Mrs Primm."

"Evening, Mr Sullivan. How are you?" I held out my hand.

He took it and gave it a firm Yorkshireman's shake.

"I'm not too bad thank you and please call me Peter."

"Oh, right, OK." We stood awkwardly for a moment, watching the party in front of us.

"Damn sorry business this thing with Bill and Beryl don't you think?"

"Yes, yes it was, tragic."

"And Vera Bailey too. Huge loss to the village old Vera."

"Yes, she was a very fine woman," I said. "I think we all miss her."

"Good friend of yours, I believe."

"Yes, I'd like to think so," I said.

"Was having a bit of a chat with Paul Barnes the other day, he was filling me on a few things that happened, strictly hush-hush you know."

"Really, I didn't think he was allowed to do that."

"Oh, don't get me wrong, he didn't tell me anything confidential. It was more to do with you, as it happens."

"Me!" I was surprised. "Why on earth would you be talking about me?"

"He was telling me that it was you that noticed Bill's barn that night. In short, that it was you that saved that girl's life. God knows how long it would have taken us to find them otherwise. Do you have any idea how many empty barns there are round here?"

"I suppose," I said. "I just wanted to find Beryl that's all."

"Well, all I know is we could do with a few more like you round here, which is why I wanted to ask you something."

"Ask away," I said.

"Well, as you know Vera ran the library as much as an informal drop in centre as anything. She wasn't meant to but it became a place where people could go to talk to someone, even if they had to pretend to be looking for a book whilst they did it."

I thought of myself and old Fred and the countless others that used to call in and see her. The kettle would go on and her time was always spared.

"Yes, I do know that. I know that only too well."

"Well, in view of the trouble we've had round here just lately, Paul was thinking we should make it officially a place that people can come to for help and advice. As much as we all like to think the problems of the big bad world aren't amongst us, we all know that to a certain extent they are, albeit on a much smaller scale."

"You mean have it as a sort of referral point, a first place of contact giving people information on where they can go to get help?"

"See, you've got the idea already."

"That seems a brilliant idea."

"Good, good, I'm glad you approve, because we'd like you to set it up and run it."

"Me, no, surely not, I don't have any experience in that kind of thing."

"Paul Barnes said he thought you were remarkable. The way you've handled the whole Bill and Beryl thing, well, most people would crack under that kind of pressure. But not you and all that on top of - how can I put this - marital difficulties," he laughed. "I think you're exactly the right person for the job."

"I don't know what to say."

"Well, have a think about it. To be honest, I hadn't meant to talk to you about it tonight. I was going to give you a call in a couple of days. But well, strike while the iron's hot and all that. I'll give you my card." He took a dog-eared card out his wallet and gave it to me.

"Right, well, thank you very much. I'm very flattered."

"There is a salary, but I'm afraid it's nothing fantastic; possibly a bit in the kitty for a couple of part timers too, but we can talk the details over when you've had a think about it. Well, I must press on. Need to rescue Mrs Sullivan from the lovely Imelda. She can't stand her."

And he disappeared.

I went immediately to find George.

"So what do you think? It's ridiculous right?"

"Not at all," said George. "I think it's a great idea."

"What, but you always said I shouldn't work, that I should be at home looking after you and Rebecca."

"Yes, I know, but that was then and this is now. The bigger question is: Do you want to do it?"

"I don't know. I suppose I do have a knack for getting my nose stuck into other people's problems."

"Well, there you go then."

"Yes, but then they die."

"Oh stop it, Jo. For once have a bit of self-belief and go out there and do something that might just make a difference to someone."

"You're right, I will. I'll do it."

So I did.

I rang Peter Sullivan and accepted the job. Within a couple of months we had it all set up: relevant agencies alerted, leaflets in place and a team of willing volunteers to help in the short term with the staffing.

We held a big open day and invited anyone and everyone to come and meet us to see what we were about.

It was hectic, but tremendous fun. Philip, George and Rebecca all pitched in serving teas, coffees and buttering scones. It felt like we were a proper family, a very unconventional family, but a family none the less.

It was as we were clearing up that the first of three unexpected things happened.

The first was when a young girl came in looking rather sheepish.

"Hi," I said. "Can I help you with something or have you just come for the open day? We've still got some tea and scones left if you'd like."

"George," I turned away to yell at him, "can you rustle up one more cuppa and a scone please, hun? Thanks."

"No, no, it's fine. I came to, well, I came to…" she paused. "You don't recognise me, do you?"

"No, I'm sorry I don't, have we me…" And then it hit me. It was her, Gemma Smith.

"Oh my God," I said. "It's you. What on earth are you doing here?"

"Please, don't be mad, I've been trying to find you for ages. It was Mr Barnes that told me about the library. He said you would be here today."

"I see."

I wasn't entirely sure how I felt about her being in Vera's library it was almost like rubbing salt into the wound, especially today. But something made me temper my mood. She looked nervous and a little afraid. Not cocky or full of attitude. No, she hadn't come here to make trouble she'd come for another reason.

I gestured to a chair, "Have a seat, are you sure I can't get you anything?"

"No, no, I'm fine, honestly, thank you."

"So what can I do for you then?" My manner was possibly a little colder than it could have been but what did she expect; she had been partly responsible for the deaths of three people.

"Well, it's just I never got a chance to say thank you for what you did that night. I know if it hadn't been for you I would have died. I just thought you should know that I appreciate it. You saved my life."

"Oh, I don't know about that. I'm sure the police would have figured it out in time."

"I'm not so sure. I knew Beryl wasn't going to kill me, but she made it very clear that my chances of getting out of there were slim. A disused barn, off the beaten track, no, Beryl may not have had the courage to kill me herself, but she made sure the odds of my living were grim."

"In God's hands, she said, but, well, I wasn't in God's hands was I? I was in yours."

"Oh, now, that's a bit dramatic..." She interrupted me.

"No, please, let me finish, I've had a lot of time to think since all this has happened. I know I have to turn my life around and make something of myself and I know I have to try and put right some of the things I have done wrong. I had no idea how much pain I was causing people, especially my parents. I really am sorry and I have changed. That's the other reason I came to see you, so I could prove it."

"Well, it's good to know something positive came out of Vera and Beryl's deaths," I said coldly.

"Look, don't misunderstand me; I do appreciate you coming out here to say thank you, but you don't have to prove anything to me. I would think it's your parents that need to hear all this."

"Oh they have, and they understand this is what I have to do and are right behind me. They think it's a great idea. Mr Barnes went to see them about it."

"See them, see them about what?" I was getting a little confused.

"About me coming to work here. Did Mr Barnes not mention it?"

I listened in disbelief to what she was telling me. Cheeky sod, how dare he.

"No, funnily enough, he didn't."

"Look," she continued, "I know you have every reason not to trust me or believe me, but don't you see that's why I need to come and work here. I know all about Vera and what she meant to people and believe me, if I could turn the clock back, I would." Her voice faltered and I saw a tear trickle from her eye.

"Please Mrs Primm, how else am I ever going to be able to live with myself if I don't try and do something good."

I handed her a tissue. "Oh, I don't know Gemma. Would it really be your kind of thing? Besides, you live in Leeds."

"Well, I can't think of anyone better to tell people the damage that drugs and drink can do than me, can you? And, to be honest, I think moving up here and getting away from all my old haunts would help keep me on the straight and narrow. Mr Barnes has given me the number of a local shared housing scheme that would help me."

"Gosh, he really does think of everything, our Mr Barnes, doesn't he?" I said sarcastically.

Mr bloody Barnes. He was like some kind of benevolent puppet master.

"Yes," said Gemma snuffling and blowing her nose. "He's very kind for a copper."

She really was a sorry sight. What would Vera do? I wondered, but actually I already knew.

"Can I think about it Gemma? I'm not saying no, but I'm not saying yes. Leave me your number and I'll let you know."

"OK, thanks." She wrote her number on a scrap of paper and I put it in a drawer.

"Bye then, thanks."

"Bye Gemma."

I sat back down at my desk, slightly baffled.

227

"Well, that was all very interesting wasn't it?" said George.

"You heard then," I said.

"Well, it was hard not to, really. We were all hiding just behind that bookshelf over there."

"She seems genuine Mum."

"I know Rebecca, but it's a tough one for me. I'll sleep on it."

"Well, we're just about done now. Washing up's finished; kitchen's cleared. Think we might be through for the day," said Philip.

"Thanks guys. You've been brilliant."

We stood in a circle and had a huge corny group hug.

"Well, I just have one or two things to finish here, so if you lot want to head off I'll catch up with you in a bit."

"We weren't going to head straight home Mum. Dad says we're going to the pub for tea."

"Oh right, OK. I guess I'll see you back at home later then." I felt forlorn and dejected. We'd had such a great day and now they were all going off to have fun and I was going home to dinner for one.

George must have seen the look of rejection on my face. "God, you can be so thick sometimes, Jo," he smiled. "'Us' means you too."

"Oh, OK, thank you."

"We'll see you down there. Don't be too long."

"I won't. Bye."

I began to tidy my desk and realised I still hadn't sorted out the morning's post.

I'll just have a quick look through, I thought. Don't want to be coming into a mess on Monday morning.

There was the usual junk mail, bills, etc. and a rather large brown paper wrapped package addressed to me, franked from Latham and Cole Solicitors in Leeds.

I assumed it was something to do with the library but it wasn't, it was from Vera's Solicitor.

Inside was a covering note which simply said.

Following the reading of Mrs Vera Bailey's will, we have been asked to pass onto you the contents of the enclosed package. We have no knowledge of what is contained in the package and therefore cannot accept responsibility for any injury or accident that may arise from opening the enclosed item.

The brown paper bundle wrapped with string. It felt from the edges like books. I cut the string gently with scissors and unwrapped it.

I knew immediately what they were. They were Vera's journals. Her whole life and thoughts set out in 20 or so little hard backed A5 notebooks. On top of them was a folded piece of paper.

My Dear Jo,

I have left these in your care because I can think of no one better to safeguard my thoughts.

There is some pretty hair-raising stuff in these books, but some stuff that will give you a laugh as well.

All I ask is that every now and again you pay my words a visit and share a cuppa with me whilst you do, nothing more.

I wish you all the happiness in the world.

Your very loving friend,

Vera.

I took the first book in my hand and flicked through the brown age-stained pages catching glimpses of her neat and very precise handwriting.

What an amazing gift. "Thank you Vera." I raised the remnant of my tea into the air.

"You get locked up for talking to yourself."

Startled, I jumped and spilt my cup of tea on my lap. I turned annoyed to see who was in the doorway, but the sun was shining directly on to its glass, the reflection masking their face.

Arse, I thought.

"Can I help you?" I said, trying not to sound pissed off. "I'm afraid the open day's finished."

He stepped through the doorway the sun now behind him so I could see who it was.

"Oh, it's you."

"Aww, why do you sound so disappointed?"

"What do you expect? You just made me spill bloody tea all over myself."

"Sorry, always did have crap timing. Can I get you a cloth?"

"No, it's fine. What are you doing here anyway? Don't tell me you've come to shut us down for illegal scone making."

He laughed.

"No, I came to see how it had all gone. Word is you're quite the heroine round here now."

"Oh yes and whose fault is that eh? No chance of keeping a low profile with you around is there? Tell you what, Max Clifford's got nothing on you mate."

"Ah yes, sorry about that, but I did think you'd thank me for putting the odd word in the right ear?"

"Well, for the record, if I'd wanted to blow my own trumpet I would have, but I didn't so you shouldn't have. Not without asking. Going round talking about me to other people; it's not on you know."

"Well, I am genuinely sorry if I upset you. I was just trying to help."

"Very well, apology accepted," I said sulkily.

"So how are you doing Jo? All joking aside."

"I'm not doing too bad DI Barnes. Thanks for asking."

I stopped tidying my desk and mopping my skirt and looked up.

"Well, I'm glad to hear it. Any chance of a cup of tea?"

"God, you policemen is that all you do all day, drink?"

"Hmm, pretty much."

"Go on then. Milk with two isn't it, same as ...."

"Bill, yeah, that's right."

I went into to the kitchen and came back to find him looking at Vera's journals.

"Err, no, please don't touch those." I went over and took the book out of his hand.

"Looks interesting, what are they?"

"Vera Bailey's journals, she left them to me in her will."

"Well, how about that, bet they'll make for interesting reading."

"Yes, I think they will."

"What is it about you and people's journals? Probably make a good book."

"Possibly. Look, is there anything else you wanted or did you just come in here for the tea and to be annoying?"

"Am I annoying?"

"Yes, very. So?"

"Well, actually there was another reason."

"Go on then."

"Well a little bird tells me that you're in charge of organising the Vera Bailey ball."

"God, you and your little birds. Yes, your bird wire is correct. What about it?"

"Well, I thought I might like to come."

"Really, OK - you do know the tickets are £35.00 each."

"Yes, I do. That's fine."

I went to get my ticket booking forms out my desk.

"So it's for two, then. Right?"

"Well, that depends."

"Depends on what?"

"On whether I can get a certain lady to be my guest."

"Right, OK, I see," I said sarcastically. "Well, perhaps you can come and get your ticket when you've asked her then." I put the book away.

"Well, that would be fine; apart from I'm not sure if she would be willing to go with me."

"Look Paul, I know we're a help centre, but I'm not sure dating advice falls into the scope of what we're here to do. Now I'm sorry I don't mean to sound rude but it's been a long day and there is a glass of wine in the bar over there with my name on it and I can hear it calling. Loudly!"

"Right, yes, of course, sorry, it's just, well..."

"Well, what? You're sounding like a love struck teenager; surely a big beefy chap like you isn't afraid of asking some woman out to a ball is he? For God's sakes man up will you, just ask her. The worst that can happen is she'll say no."

"Yes, you're right. Man up. God, I always was rubbish at this kind of thing."

He paused and took a deep breath.

"Mrs Primm, would you do me the honour of accompanying me to The Vera Bailey Memorial Ball?"

"You're joking, right?"

"No, no I'm not."

"Why on earth would you want to do that?"

"Because I like you."

"Oh, please you hardly know me."

"No, but I've seen enough to believe you are one of the cleverest, funniest, most beautiful woman I have ever met."

"You need to get out more," I was gob smacked.

"Seriously Jo, I haven't been able to stop thinking about you."

"Me! God you must be bored."

"See! This is why I knew it was a bad idea, I'm sorry, I shouldn't have said anything. I'll go."

He put his cup down and made for the door.

"No stop," I called. "I'm sorry, it's me; sarcasm you see. It's my first line of defence in situations of a shocking, unpredictable, previously unencountered nature. I'm truly stunned you would want to."

"Well, will you?"

"Can I think about it?" He looked disappointed.

What was I thinking, of course I should go with him.

"Tell you what," I said. "I'll let you know when we go for a drink next week."

I got out my diary. "Any day better for you?"

"Well I'm free on Monday, does that suit?"

"Yep, that seems fine. You can pick me up at 7.30pm."

"Whatever you say, Jo. You're the boss."

Fancy another cracking read?

A broken marriage and tragedy in his past; Mark Kemp
is in a sorry state by the time he reaches the old
tenement close known as "Starlings' Yard".

Taking inspiration from the dark atmosphere and the
strangeness of the people, he begins to paint again, only to
discover that he has unwittingly become a resident in a place
whose past and present hide dark and sinister secrets.

Readers' Reviews

"This is a clever novel which works on a number of levels. It is
easy to get into and much harder to put down. It captures you
and awakens old memories and fears. Brilliant."

...

"Dingy old slums, ghosts and gangsters combine to make
this sinister plot come alive beneath the dark under belly of
Edinburgh. Any aspiring artist can't fail to connect with our
hero. The description of the artist at work can't fail to inspire."